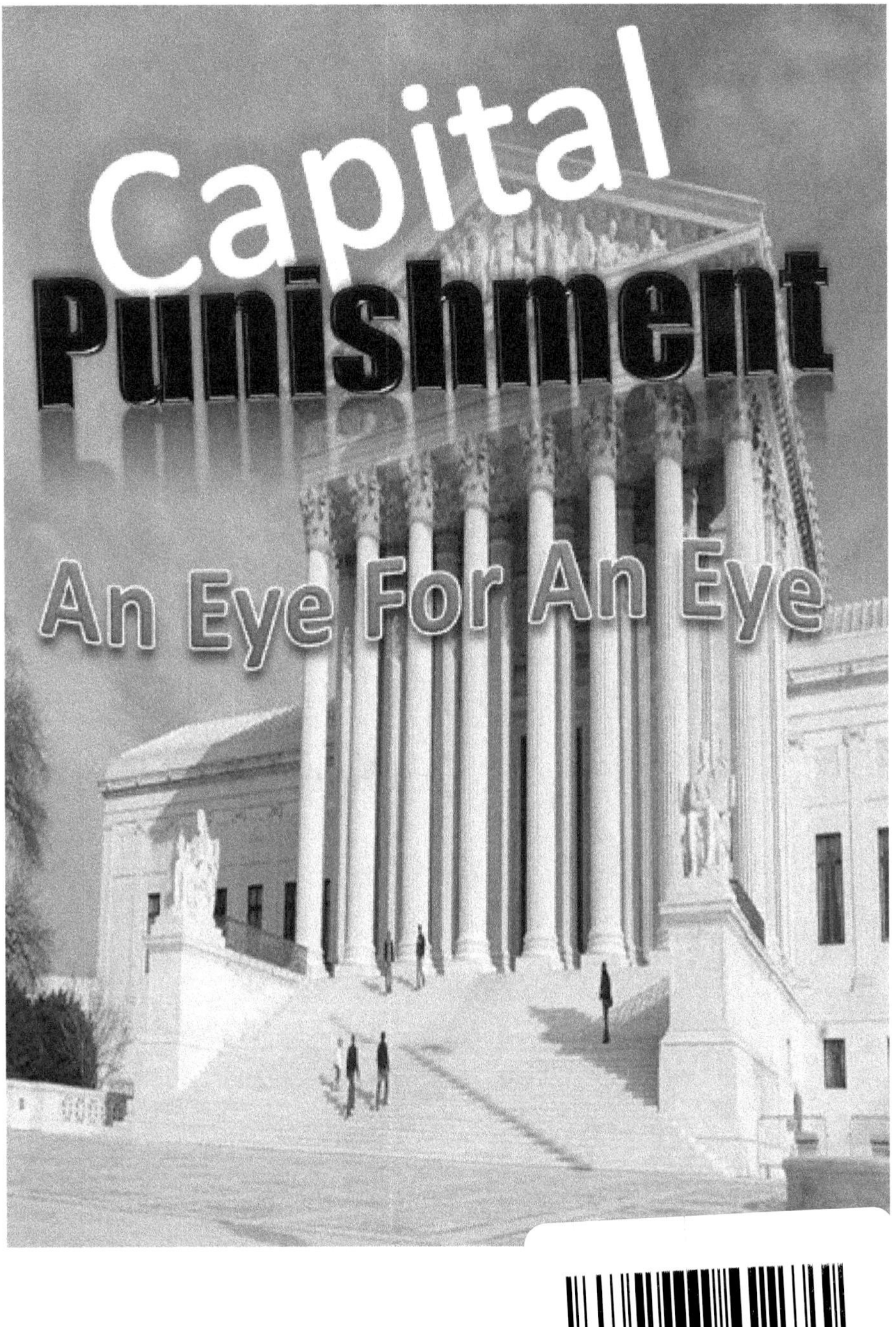

Capital Punishment

An Eye For An Eye

Capital Punishment

An Eye

For

An Eye

By

Tom Cooke

If you had a way to prevent crime or turn evil into good, would you be willing to buck the system?

Author's Note

This book is a work of fiction as all names, places, events, characters, companies, and incidents are intended to be fictitious and a product of the Author's imagination and any resemblance to actual persons or events are purely coincidental.

License Notes

Acknowledgements

I would like to thank my wife, Sandy, for the many hours she spent alone in front of the TV while I was on the computer.

Also, thank you for not pushing the "honey do's" that hopefully will now get done. I would also like to thank my kids who always encouraged me to finish this book for over a century: well, it languished from one century (1986) to the next (2013). "What happened to that book you were writing?" This was the question presented time and time again?

Finally, shamed to the point I had to do something, I dug it out of the closet and was determined to finish it. Stalled once again to the care of Sandy, who then went home to be with the Lord in May 2018, and several years rebuilding my life after 60 years together, I am ready to finish this.

Thanks, again, for the never ending prodding, support and comfort.

Dedication

"Dedicated to my wife, Sandy, and my children—whose love, support, and presence shape the person I am today.

Without you, this journey would be incomplete."

Book Page Layout

Table of Contents

Table of Contents

Introduction

The world is inundated with crime. Punishment is failing to deter criminals. The justice system is nothing but a revolving door for criminals who know how to play the system.

Henry Mulenbeck's wife is brutally raped and murdered. Henry sets out to avenge her death through a system of "equal punishment" for the crime. Henry Mulenbeck, a Research and Development expert in the field of Functioning Apparatus sets out to level the playing field. Through the development of "CloBots" his success has been overwhelming. CloBots, administering equal justice, have put fear into anyone who would consider crime.

After a period of time his success is heralded nationwide and crime seems to be a thing of the past.

Or, is it?

Like everything in life, "nothing is a sure thing." Crime once again emerges. Only, this time it has taken an uncanny twist.

What can be done to overcome the perfect crime? Or, the perfect criminal?

Chapter One

The Celebration

In life there are adversaries. The hunter and the hunted! The predator and the victim! The predator is driven. The victim is unaware. The predator is driven by the need of the hunt: driven by the need of life's necessities. Most of all he is driven by the need of fulfillment. The victim is innocent. The victim is living life, hopefully unmolested. Instinct initiates the predator's hunt. Love of life consumes the victim. That is the basic nature of the animal kingdom.

The last two years have been remarkable. Remarkable, yet hectic! Things were moving so fast that, at one point, it gave new meaning to "Living life in the fast lane." There was graduation, a new job, a girlfriend, marriage, and on and on. However, now life is starting to slow down as things are finally settling down and coming together. I am more than ready to take that "slow boat to China."

Today is a day of celebration and we, my beautiful wife, Carol, and I, are more than ready.

We are ready because this past year has been a year of hard work for both of us. Our jobs are very demanding, requiring a lot of overtime. Overtime! Who wants it? Yeah, many like it for the extra dollars. But is it worth the time that it robs you of the things and people you love? However, we can't complain because we knew what was demanded in these job positions when we were hired. Was it our smartest moves? Time will tell!

Today, Carol and I are celebrating our first wedding anniversary. It was one year ago today, June 14, 2042 that Carol and I said, "I do." One year ago, on that unforgettable, wonderful, amazing day. I was in Heaven as we said our vows to one another. "Do you take….?" Those words keep ringing in my ears like an angel's harp. It's beautiful music, a tune that I will sing over and over for the rest of my life. Now, today, Friday June 14, 2043, we will celebrate the 365th day of our Honeymoon. My name is Henry Mulenbeck; most people call me "Hank." I am married to the most beautiful woman on this, or any other planet in the Universe.

The animal kingdom from top to bottom of the food chain is born with certain instincts. Creation has instilled in it the basic instincts for survival. These instincts, which are honed throughout life, are for the preservation and propagation of the species.

I was attracted to Carol Adams the first time I saw her at W.O.S.E. Carol is a tall, slender, super sexy brunette with large hazel eyes. Carol had just been hired at the same company where I was employed. She was hired as a Computer Programmer. I was on break, in the break room, when Carol came in. I tried to be casual as we were introduced by my best friend, but I am sure my expressions gave me away: I was captivated. I was head over heels "in love at first sight." What a dumb-dumb that said, "there is no such thing." Truth be told, I was probably drooling all over myself.

Somebody better get me a towel.

I think Carol was also impressed with this six-foot-three athlete, who could have gone "pro" but chose a career in Aeronautics instead. Not wanting to take any chances of someone beating me to the punch, I jumped into uncharted waters and immediately asked if she would like to have coffee or something sometime? We began dating almost immediately. Although I could have married her the day we met, I constrained myself about asking her for a whole three months. Then, amazingly, she said yes.   We were married exactly one year after that first date: which also produced our first kiss.   I still haven't forgotten it: even though it was just a polite, thank you, goodnight peck, I tucked it away to sustain me until our first real kiss - two weeks later.

Actually, we are celebrating a double anniversary tonight. It was, also two years ago today that I landed one of the most coveted jobs in the computer industry. After graduating at at the top of my class at one of the most respected colleges in science and engineering, I was offered a position in the General Research & Development Department at World Organization of Space Exploration, Inc. (WOSE). After a year with WOSE, I was offered a higher position in the Deep Space Habitation and Exploration (DSHE) department, which we now call DeeSHE).

Instincts are aroused and the predator is on the move. So, now the hunt begins. There is a need for a hunt, and the need must be fulfilled. Need always arouses the instincts. Moving, searching, he knows the territory well, for he has been here or other places like it many times before.

My current job at WOSE, in DeeShe, is to research and develop Functioning Apparatus Systems for deep space exploration and habitation. This is for future missions of deep space explorations and habitation before the end of the next decade. It is amazing what we have accomplished since man blasted off into space just over eighty years ago. And, now, I have been a part of it for the last two years, making every grueling hour spent in what seems a lifetime of studies well worth it. These have been two years doing what I love, working in the most exciting and self-rewarding job a man can do. I hope to spend my entire career working here, together with Carol, of course, at WOSE.

Carol just called and said she is now leaving work, after having to work overtime to try and finish a project, which she didn't, and that means more overtime. I told her to tell them this is cruel and unusual punishment to do to someone on their first wedding anniversary. She did. It didn't make any difference: she had to stay.

I am glad our anniversary has fallen on a Friday because that will give us all weekend to celebrate. There is nothing better than a long slow celebration. We, also, will be adding a mini-celebration to our already dual celebration: six months in our new home in Houston's prestigious "upper-crust" neighborhood: "The Northsides." This is one of those environmentally efficient, easy-living, and gated communities. It is located just off the outer belt on the northwest side of Houston. Our home sits at 14001 Cedar Crest Road. It is a beautiful 4500 square foot home with four large bedrooms, each with its own bathroom (which we intend to fill with children: just as soon as things really settle down). There is also a visitor's bathroom on the first floor and a huge family room with floor to ceiling windows on one wall overlooking a forest of trees to keep all neighbors separated. We have the most modern of kitchens, and a library, again, with floor to ceiling windows and a full wall of book shelves. We also have a kidney-shaped pool out back and a humongous patio with a large fire pit. I am working with the elite, living with the elite and most of all married to the most "Elite."

Now, as soon as Carol gets here with the steaks, which she is picking up on her way home from the office, "The Celebrations" will begin. And, we intend to make the most of it. In fact, it is not going to be just a one night celebration but I intend for it to last all weekend! Friday for our wedding anniversary, Saturday for our jobs celebration, and Sunday for the purchase of our new house celebration. "Hummm..." Let's see if we can find something for Monday? I'm sure we could squeeze another day off - the flu is very contagious this time of year!

My best friend Steve Harrison, who works in the same department at WOSE as I, gave me a bottle of Egly-Ouriet Brut Tradition Grand Cru champagne for our wedding anniversary: which will be the perfect celebrations. Steve is not only my best friend but he was also the Best Man at our wedding and the one who had introduced me to Carol that fateful day in the break room. That is why inexpensive champagne would never be suitable for his two dear friends. Steve was well aware of our expensive tastes: he, having also been my roommate for the last two years in college, living on pizza and greasy hamburgers.

Crouching beneath the cover of the tall grass, the predator waits. A smart predator always seeks to be hidden. Lack of cover will lead to exposure. Exposure will lead to termination: not of a prey but of a hunt. Waiting, patiently, always brings its rewards. An impatient, restless predator will always spook his intended victim.

Getting here wasn't easy, though. It seems that I have spent my whole life on schooling and job training programs. As far back as I can remember, it was school, school, and more school. My parents are Joel and Gretta Mulenbeck Jr. who, came here from Germany. My mother was a German citizen and my father a German Jew from America. They both were very poor in the beginning and felt that the only way to get ahead in life was through education and hard work. So, little "Hank" was marched off to pre-school at the ripe age of four to start my formal education.

Unlike many children starting school with one or both parents who were immigrants and some who continued to speak their native language in their homes and in public, I had already learned to speak English. My mother, an immigrant, was a teacher in the old country and was fluent in English as well as German. She met my father shortly after he arrived in Germany for his final two years in the Army. My father, having been raised in the "good ol'" USA did not speak German, so when he met this beautiful German girl at the USO, he knew he had to get to know her. Using awkward made up sign language to communicate in German; he spent about five minutes trying to ask her to dance. He could tell by the smile on her face she, too, was interested. When she couldn't stand it any longer she said to him,

"I would love to dance with you." They both couldn't help but laugh.

It was a match made in Heaven. They fell in love and were married six months later.

Upon the completion of his tour of duty they returned to his home in New York City, New York: Long Island, to be exact. I was six months old, born May 21, 2018, when we arrived at "Papa's" home two days before

Christmas.

He has fixed upon a scent in the air. It is a scent that triggers all the tools necessary within the predator to fulfill the hunt. The stalking of his prey is a matter of utmost skills. One wrong move and this hunt is over. The predator must draw on everything he has learned in previous hunts so that not only instinct but experience will produce a victim. Now, he must continue to remain absolutely undetected so the victim will never know what hit him.

Papa's home was the home of his parents who had immigrated here right after WWII. My grandparents left the home to Papa when they decided to return to the old country after grandma got very ill and was not expect to live long. She died shortly after returning to Germany. This was several years before I was born.

Momma continued her career as a

teacher. She loved children, even though she was only able to have one child: yours truly.

The home was one of the post war larger "ranch" style houses built in 1949 in Levittown. The suburbs were the place to be. They were springing up everywhere with their own schools, parks, and shopping centers: a migration from the big city. My grandfather, Joel Mulenbeck Sr., a World War II holocaust survivor, was a proud man who worked hard and gave his children a chance at the new life in America. Papa learned well from his father.

Papa also felt that his children should have the same opportunities his father had given him. But Papa also learned that opportunity may only "knock once," so you must be prepared to grab hold, and being prepared only comes through education and hard work. Throughout my elementary, junior, and high school years, I was required to maintain a very rigid schedule: up early in the morning to do morning chores, have breakfast, and then off to school. After school, it was "Homework Time" until dinner, no "IFs," "Ands," or "Buts." After dinner and clean-up, including dishes, and taking out the trash, it was time for "Papa" to look over and check out my homework. If all wasn't finished and done correctly, it was done over again.

I grew up in a very strict home with many rules that were not to be broken, or there would be consequences that, by today's standards, would not be permitted. But, it was also a home filled with love.

Papa adored Momma and they both loved me and told me so, daily. Yes, there were strictness and the many rules, some of which I thought were unnecessary. However, as I look back, I wouldn't want anything to have been different: without them, I don't believe I would be the person I am today!

> *A herd has been spotted. Here he will find his victim! The herd begins to move. Now, the stalking begins. Quietly the predator is laying out his plan, waiting for just the right moment to attack. One of the basic skills of a predator is patience: without it the hunt is in jeopardy! Stalking your prey is a matter of both skill and patience. A spooked prey is a prey that will live for another day. The stalking of the prey is coming to a finish, and the end is in sight. The hunt is reaching its climax: an unaware victim is just moments from drawing its last breath.*

Finally, graduation time came and I was very proud of what I had accomplished; with the help of Papa, of course. I was chosen Valedictorian for the class of 2036. And the fact that I was graduating with a 4.0 grade point average, and the only kid in school with a perfect attendance record, did not make me a "nerd." I also played football, the team's quarterback, who set a school record for scored touchdowns. But, baseball was my favorite: "one heck'a first baseman," if I must say so myself. I had a scholarship in both academics and sports. I continued playing baseball throughout college, but my mind was still concentrating on my academics. I guess it's true: "You raise a child up in the right way, and when he is old, he will not depart." Papa did his job well!

I was very proud, not only of myself but of "Papa," for his determination that I would not only make it through but make it through on top. I was also very proud of Momma for she was there standing behind me, with words of praise and support, as Papa guided me through many tough times. Papa felt that "there were many who do, but that there are only a few who do well." I graduated from high school and I felt that I had "done well."

Then it was off to college. Success was achieved once again, this time with Papa behind me, not over me as he was when I was a child.

Papa had plenty of time to support me starting with my junior year because Momma, who had developed breast cancer, died at the end of my freshman year. It was very difficult to concentrate on my studies as I grieved for Momma and tried my best to care for Papa. Papa was lost after that, and I was all he had left. But Papa would have none of it. He knew that life must go on and that I, as well as he, must look to the future: the immediate future for us and an eternal future with Momma.

Standing behind me (I think this was Papa's way of assuring me Momma was still there supporting me), Papa was supporting, helping and encouraging me in every way possible. I graduated from college with the same accolades as from high school, which helped earn my present position at WOSE.

Out in front of him is one of the important essentials of life: not only his life, but the life of those that depend on him. Life must be sustained. The predator waits! The opportunity to pounce and capture his intended prey is a matter of perfect timing, and he knows that that time is drawing near.

Well, the coals in the BBQ are "white hot," and just in time, I heard the garage door opener kick on and the door going up. A million things run through your mind as you try to be prepared for the second most perfect night of your life (the first, naturally, being your wedding night). Is the lighting just right? Where are the champagne glasses? Did I overdo the aftershave? Will she like her anniversary gift? On and on, these thoughts raced through my head. You set the stage a million times in your mind of what a night like this will be. Over and over, you play out the scene, even to the very dialog you might carry on.

I also played out the scene that it would be great if Papa could see me now. His son celebrating his first wedding anniversary and celebrating two years at this fantastic job. Papa would be busting his proud buttons! Papa died of a massive heart attack two months after Carol and I were married. Papa's spirit, his zest for life, will always be with us.

I wonder what is taking Carol so long. She shouldn't have had but one, maybe two small bags of last-minute shopping items for our celebration. Here, pouring champagne in one of the special anniversary glasses, I'll surprise her with a glass of champagne when she steps through the door. That will take the edge off all the stress from her day at work and the unexpected overtime.

Animals also have a brain, personalities, and emotions. New studies are revealing that they have feelings of emotions, such as sorrow or moodiness. They also show anger! However, in the lower animal kingdom, anger is not associated with pleasure but only with survival. Rarely do they ever stray beyond these instincts unless diseased! And a diseased animal is a danger, both to his kingdom and the kingdom of other species.

Finally, the door from the kitchen to the garage opens. I look with anticipation and excitement for her beautiful face to appear. A porcelain face with skin so soft and smooth. A heavenly face with a smile that only an Angel could know. A happy face: with a smile that not only lights up her face but causes your face to light up in response. This is the face I was waiting to see!

I held my breath! Feeling anxious, waiting for this moment, my heart began pounding faster and faster. I remembered that this was the same reaction I had the first time I met Carol. I better check and make sure I am not drooling!

My heart and my thoughts were racing as I was waiting to be greeted by Carol's smile and to see her anticipation of beginning our night of celebration, which she expressed in her last words on the phone.

There, there it is! One has been singled out. Unwisely straying from the protection of the herd, it has become very vulnerable. The choice has been made. The predator has his intended victim within his grasps. It is now defenseless to the predator! The perfect moment has arrived. Springing from its cover, with the power and speed of a locomotive, the strike was precise and deadly. The hunter had stalked, attacked, and subdued his prey. It is nature unsurpassed. The survival of the fittest!

The door opens slowly and Carol begins to appear. The moment has arrived: "let the celebration begin."

"There she is. That beautiful, happy face I've been longing to see. Wait! I don't understand! Instead of the

Angelic smile, as Carol comes through the door, she has a look on her face that I have never seen before. It appeared to be a look of confusion. Her smile was absent. Her face seemed distorted, perplexed! I didn't understand what I was seeing because Carol was well aware of the situation: the celebration, and we both could hardly wait to get started.

As she stepped farther into the room I saw that it was not confusion, but a look of TERROR! FEAR! And UNBELIEF! Carol was having a hard time processing what was happening. I was having a hard time processing what was causing Carol to look like this: a look I have never seen before.

Stepping in behind Carol was a man who looked as if he had just crawled out of the sewer. He looked like he had been homeless for a long time and hadn't bathed or changed clothes in months. His hair was one big ball of grease. His eyes were cold black. They had no color to them, and there were only very large "pupils." It seemed that you could look straight into this person's soul and see what he is made of, and it wasn't good. Hatred! Anger! Evil!

Man, who is the preeminent crowning achievement of creation, is not limited to instincts. Yes, man has the instinct for survival but he also has the capacity for much more. Man has a soul. Man's soul consists of a mind, emotions, and a will. With these additional traits man can reason, interact intelligently, calculate, choose, and establish meaningful relationships. Relationships beyond instinct require a soul: the ability to love, think and choose. Man is a communal creature.

He looked as if he hadn't slept for a "month of Sundays," judging from the bags under his eyes. His clothes appeared as though they hadn't been in a washing machine for months and months and had many holes in them. In his one hand was a gun, which was stuck in Carol's ribs and in the other hand, what appeared to be a hunting knife, which he brought up to her throat.

"Who are you? What do you want?" I could barely whisper, due to my shock at seeing Carol like this.

"You can have anything you want, our money, our jewelry, here; you can have the keys to my car." I frantically dug into my pocket to get the keys to give to him.

Please, just leave us alone!" I pleaded as I stepped forward to hand him the keys.

"Just shut-up man, and get back," he blurted out.

"O.K., but just take the stuff and leave us alone," I pleaded, once again.

"You just don't get it, do you man?" he sneered. "I'm in charge here. I'm the one calling the shots. You'll do what I say, when I say it. Now, SIT DOWN!" he shouted, waving the gun toward the couch.

I went and sat down, knowing that he meant it and hoping that if I did as he said he would take the stuff and go. But something deep inside me said that that was not going to happen. I could see the coldness in his eyes and the total disregard for others and their feelings or even their life.

He then ordered Carol to get some of her nylons and tie me up. He warned her she had thirty seconds to return or he would "blow my head off." Carol and I both knew she had no choice except to do exactly as he said. Carol knew she had to be back within thirty seconds, or he would take the most pleasure in doing just what he threatened to do.

Carol was back in a flash with a hand full of her undergarments. Trembling, almost to the point that she could hardly stand, she held them out to him. He just looked at her as if he were disappointed she made it back on time. He ordered her to tie my wrist and legs and that "it had better be done right."

With tears streaming down her face, she did what he commanded. I just wanted to reach out and grab Carol, hold her, and never let go. I could see the pain in her eyes as she had to tie me up instead of caressing me.

Man's survival is not intended to be a confrontation of anger and destruction. Man's "survival of the fittest" is a rise to the top through knowledge and hard work. But, somehow, some have polluted themselves and greed and pleasure have become their instinct for survival, anger being the fuel to sustain their existence. Man has become diseased! Man has become like a diseased animal, no longer acting according to his nature. He has lost the capacity for relationships; his soul is no longer capable of communal existence. He, too, has become a predator! He is now a danger to his species, as well as, all creation.

This was supposed to be our night of celebration. This was the night we were to hold and love one another. Instead it has turned into a nightmare!

Carol now had to do an unthinkable task of binding the one she loved. There was a pleading in her eyes that I could not do anything to relieve. My heart was breaking as tears were streaming down both our faces.

Knowing that she could not tie me up sufficiently so that I could not escape, He ordered Carol to sit on the floor across the room so she could watch what this animal was doing as he took much pleasure in tormenting the both of us. He then came over and skillfully bound my hands and legs, making each knot as if he were trying to earn a "scout badge." All the while, Carol was frantically pleading for him not to hurt us. All he would do was mutter, "Don't worry about your little man, sweetie

The prey is down. It is now meat for survival. There will be nothing left. Complete destruction and consumption of the prey is the only objective. Anything less is unthinkable to the predator. His needs will have been supplied.

Then my worst fears became reality. He turned and grabbed Carol, dragging her into the bedroom, saying, "See, I told you, you don't have to worry about your little man." I was only about fifteen feet away, and I was totally helpless to go to Carol's aid. All I could do was sit there bound, gagged, and listen to Carol as she begged and pleaded for mercy.

I struggled and struggled in vain to free myself from the bindings, only to have them cut deep into my wrists. As I struggled to get free, I could see their shadows on the bedroom wall. The sight made me sick to my stomach. I could see his figure above hers. I could hear his....moaning, as he was having his way with her. Moaning, with what was supposed to be an act of love and adoration between two people. Moaning, as he was stealing the act that was supposed to belong to only Carol and me. Moaning, as he violated this sanctimonious act of love with his "animalistic" devouring of his prey.

The rage welled up in me. I could feel my blood heating to almost the boiling point. Yet, I was still helpless as a child, bound by these restraints, as the tears streamed down my face, and I cried out to God for mercy.

It seemed like an eternity, the shadows dancing on the wall. Suddenly, with a lot of motion and loud moaning on his part, it was over, and the only sound was the muffled cries of

Carol as he was apparently holding his hand over her mouth. Her cries were like those of a baby, one whose heart had just been broken because someone had scared it to death.

Then, just as I had hopes this horrible nightmare was coming to an end, I realized that it had just began. Once again, I saw his shadow rise above Carol, and his hand was high in the air above Carol. He paused as if he knew that, on the wall, I was getting a "black and white" TV picture of all that was happening. Then his hand came down with a thud. His hand rose over and over, thrusting downward again and again. I thought, "Oh, no…he is beating her." I then could make out the outline on the wall, and it was not a fist, but something was in his hand.

My GOD! He had the knife. He was stabbing Carol! I could hear a sickening thud over and over as he plunged the knife into Carol's body.

"Oh, my God, he is killing her. He's killing my…my Carol." I tried to scream, but only a muffled whimper could be heard.

I struggled and struggled with all my might to get free. I could feel the bindings cutting deeper into my wrist as I felt the warmth of blood running down my hands. I would even have cut my hands off with the bindings if I could have, but as I was struggling, I could see it was over.

Carol's moaning and cries, as she cried out my name again and again, pleading for help, began to get weaker and weaker, until there was nothing but silence. A silence that you would never dream existed. A silence that overtook the rage and muffled the crying out of my whole being to help her. A silence that went far beyond any human emotion to produce emptiness in me: that even the noise from a roaring Super Bowl crowd would be unheard.

After conquering his prey, the predator fulfills his basic needs for survival. He then supplies the needs of the dependent ones. Nature has once again acted with precision!

At last it was over. Carol's suffering, her pain, her torment, her humiliation, all came to an end. Now, at last, she could be at peace, no longer having to suffer at the hands of this animal. No, he is far worse than an animal. No animal would do what he just did in the name of "pleasure." An animal would only kill out of fear or for survival. This..., this..., maniac, this sub human did all this in the name of "pleasure." He seems to thrive on the suffering he inflicted on Carol. He is diseased! He is a madman!

There he stood in the doorway. He stood tall and proud as if he had just conquered the world. Defiant: to all that is right and decent. The epitome of inhumanity displayed. The ultimate of what one human being can do to destroy another. There he stood, covered with the blood of one who would never dream of harming another. There he stood, licking at the drops of Carol's blood that had splattered on his face. Still after her death he was trying to violate her even further.

There is pleasure in all of God's creation. The lower animal takes pleasure in sustenance and procreation. Man takes pleasure in knowing he has done well, helped others, and served his creator. This is intended pleasure. Only the diseased or corrupted takes pleasure in selfish lust, greed, or evil desires.

There he stood. He laughed! All this time, his eyes were fixed on mine. He wanted to let me know he is now "the man." I just prayed that he would kill me and get it over with and I could then be with Carol to assure her everything was alright.

I looked at him with all the hatred any human could muster toward another for what he had just done. But, even with my desire for revenge and the hate I could muster up to express that desire; it was no match for the way he looked at me. His eyes were deep set and cold black. Looking into his eyes, you could see there was only a little white showing around what appeared to be big black round holes that let the evil in and the hatred and destruction out.

These were eyes that reflected a mind that was totally void of any human qualities. A mind captivated by another source. His eyes were a picture window to this monster's soul. These eyes were empty of any human qualities. Haunting! Demonic!

Again, he laughed. He started toward me, moving ever so slowly as if to prolong the agony. Waving the knife, stained with the blood of my love, he moved closer and closer, jabbing out at me over and over, teasing, yet letting me know that at any second it all could be over.

"Kill me!" My mind screamed out as I tried to utter the words. I choked on the gag he had stuffed so tightly halfway down my throat.

As he approached, he seemed to hear or read my thought.

"No, my man, I'm not going to kill you. That would be too easy for you." He seemed to be playing some kind of guessing game with me. "Yeah, you would like me to get it over with, wouldn't you?" he sneered. "Your pain will be far greater than your pretty little lady's was."

A diseased animal may kill because of its disease, but its actions and performance are due to its instinct for survival: it is not out of pleasure. A diseased human performs these animalistic acts in the name of pleasure. These people are no longer human: they have become lower than an animal.

All the while he was playing his sick little game I struggled to get free so I could get my hands on him, all to no avail.

Pointing the knife toward the bedroom, he sneered, "Hey man, be happy, hers was fast compared to yours. No! I want to be sure that yours last a long, long time" he muttered.

Then as quick as the strike of a serpent, he slashed out with the knife, and I felt the flesh burn from the top of my cheek to my chin.

Stooping down to admire his work, he said, "There, now, when you look in the mirror, in case you forget, I've made sure you will have something to remember this day as long as you live." I immediately had the thought that it will be a lot longer than you will, once I get free. Then, with a little snicker he continued, "Or, maybe I should just carve M. T. across your forehead." He snarled as he stroked the knife across my forehead, as if he were writing, just barely scratching the flesh. "That way, you will remember my name when you see it" he whispered.

He moved in so close, that I could even feel hate, like a fire, in his awful breath. All I could do sit there and listen as he thoroughly enjoyed himself at humanities expense. But I didn't just sit there like some beaten animal. I mustered up every ounce of hate I could and let it boil to overflowing as I fixed my stare on him.

"Oh, yes! I can see the hate in your eyes. You would like to be free so you can get even with me, huh man?" he mocked. "You could get off, just like I did with your little lady. You just want to take me down, don't you?" he screamed.

Once again, it was like he was reading my thoughts.

"An 'eye for an eye,' man. I bet that's what you want!" Laughing, he stood up, backed away one step and sensing that I wanted loose to do to him what he had just done to Carol, he said "No, I can't do that man; if I let you go, then I would have to kill you!"

That is the last thing I remembered as I saw him kick out, and I felt his boot land alongside my temple once, twice,....I lost count as I lost consciousness from the blows.

This disease, shown by this sub-human, has just reached the epitome of depravity! Just as a diseased animal must be dealt with and removed that others may survive, so too, this disease on society must be eradicated!

Chapter Two

Consciousness

I could hear ringing. It sounded so far away, so, so far away. Faint, as if, it's just my imagination. Then it stopped. Again, there was the ringing sound. It stopped again. What seemed like an eternity, then there was some sort of dull thud, again and again. Everything seemed so, so far away, but somehow, I felt it was near.

The pattern continues, first the ringing then the pounding. Both far, far away: but, seeming to get closer. As it seemed to be getting closer and closer I realized that the pounding was no longer in my head but coming from somewhere else. With that realization, I knew that I was waking up: I was regaining consciousness. Had I been asleep, and this pain in my head and the memories that are flooding into my head, had it all been a dream? Or, was it a nightmare? As I became more and more alert, still weak from the loss of blood and this pain in my head from the beating, I realized it had not been a dream or nightmare but that it was someone at the front door.

"Oh, God, please don't leave," I tried to utter, but, again choking from the gag in my mouth.

"Hank, Hank!" Were the calls as the pounding on the door got more intense and louder?

"Where are you guys?" A voice seeped through the door. "Party times over, time to get back to the real world." I heard, in what seemed to be a familiar voice.

As the pattern, of calling out and pounding on the door continued, I began to recognize the voice; it was my best friend Steve. Steve and his girlfriend, Maddisen, always came by early Saturday mornings so we could go to the gym for an early workout, and the girls could go shopping. They probably hesitated today, knowing that it was our anniversary celebration weekend. Today, they gave us what they thought was a couple more hours of time together, so they waited until almost noon.

Once their needs have been provided, there is satisfaction: until hunger, threat, or survival once again becomes a necessity or responsibility.

I know you're in there. What's going on? What are you doing?" He kept yelling, almost with a naughty suggestion in his voice.

I tried to make some noise, to move or kick and knock something over, but every nerve in my body seemed to be on fire from the beating, which I found out later was not just to my head. Then there was silence.

"Oh, no, they're leaving!" I thought, as the tears started running down my cheeks. I knew if they left, I would die. "Please, please, don't go!"

After what seemed like forever, I heard the tumblers in the lock turning and I remembered Steve knew about the hidden key in the fake rock in the flower bed along the porch.

Steve opened the door ever so cautiously, expecting to catch us in the act of something he wasn't supposed to see. As the door opened wide enough, he caught a glimpse of me curled up on the floor in a pool of blood. My eyes were set on his, pleading for help.

"Oh, my God, what happened?" He screamed as he ran to my side. He tore at the bindings and the gag, sending pain from even his lightest touch through every cell in my body. Finally, sensing my pain with his every touch and being as careful as possible, he was able to remove the gag from my mouth.

"Carol!" I tried to scream, but only my lips would move, and no sound would come out. Again, I tried to scream with all my might; I said, "Carol." That was all I could faintly utter as I once again blacked out. I would drift in and out of consciousness, pleading for them to help Carol and assure me that everything was alright.

The next thing I heard, as I once again drifted back into consciousness, was screams coming from the bedroom. Horrible, blood-curdling screams! Ear-piercing cries of horror, from both Steve and Maddisen, who had gone in to the bedroom to check on Carol, as I had pleaded for them to do.

Steve had met Maddisen Mayberry at our wedding reception. She is the daughter of the main receptionist at WOSE. Like Carol and I, they, too, felt an immediate attachment and have grown to love one another. They plan to be married next spring. She and Carol have become best friends: no, a bond much deeper than that, they are like sisters.

"Oh, God, no, no!" Steve cried out and I could hear Maddisen screaming and sobbing uncontrollably in the background.

Again, I blacked out. When I came to, the place was swarming with people. There were people in many different types of uniforms and street clothes. There were several in white uniforms attending to me as they placed me on a stretcher.

Several different police officers would come to ask questions but would be sent away by the person who seemed to be in charge of the medical team.

"No questions now, please!" he exclaimed, "This man cannot talk to anyone right now!"

My mind was fighting to tell him I must answer their questions: NOW! I must talk to them now so that they can catch that bastard who did this. However, my body did not have enough strength left to resist.

Responsibility is not driven by anger but by need. Anger is driven not by need but by greed. Needs are the necessities of life. Greed is the gluttony of not only life's necessities but also its lust and pleasures. Only man can destroy, with pleasure his intended purpose.

The next thing I really remember, other than a lot of strange faces, was waking up in the hospital room to see Steve. Steve was very nervous and distraught, pacing back and forth. When Steve saw I was awake, he rushed to the bedside and, with his trembling hand, took my hand and tried to comfort me, not realizing that I was still in a fog and not sure of what plane of reality I was on. It all still seems like a bad dream or nightmare. My mind was in a thick, heavy fog. It was as if I had been on a week-long binge and it was difficult to get my thoughts back in order or to touch sobriety.

Totally unsure of the situation, I said to Steve, "What's going on?" Somewhere, in the back of my mind, I struggled to get a hold on reality. I knew that if this were just some sort of a nightmare that my body would not be hurting from head to toe, the way it is.

Steve realized then that I still didn't have my feet on the ground. "It's Monday." Steve said.

I tried to think, I could only say, "Monday?". What was the last thing I remember? I was waiting for Carol to get home for our wedding celebra....Oh,

God, was it a nightmare? Or, was it real?

"Where is Carol?" I said as fear once again welled up, engulfing my whole being.

"Carol!"

"CAAROLLLL!!!" I screamed, as I tried to get out of bed to find her.

My thoughts were racing a hundred, a hundred-thousand miles a minute. I looked at Steve, my eyes pleading for answers. Steve looked as puzzled as I as he turned away: he, too, not wanting to face reality.

My head, spinning like a top, began to slow down and my thoughts began to clear up and I came to the realization of what really had happened. I finally realized that it had been no dream and that it wasn't a nightmare. At this realization, all I could do was cry uncontrollably. I know that the pain of a "heart attack" could not compare with the pain my heart felt as I once again lived that brutal night over and over in my mind.

Steve sat there on the side of my bed just holding my hand and crying with me for what seemed the entire night. He tried to console me with words, but the words just would not come: there weren't any words that could help. There are no words; there is no consolation when you have just been through what I went through. He not only considered Carol a dear friend but grew to lover her as if she were his own sister. Steve was deeply suffering too.

Throughout the night we cried then talked, then cried a little more.

Talking seemed to help as it became clear in my head what really happened. Knowing that, gave me the realization of what I really had to deal with.

I told Steve, "I will never forget the face and the laughing of that monster who called himself 'M. T'. And, I will never forget his parting words "An eye for an eye, man."

That is when I promised myself and Carol, "Yes! One day, 'an eye for an eye'."

Has the lower kingdom now risen higher than creations crowning achievement? Pleasure is not what drives the predator, who is strictly in survival mode. Unnatural pleasures reside only in the predator who is acting outside his kingdom element.

After another three days, I was released from the hospital, although, still in quite a bit of pain. But in order to keep the promise I made to Carol, I knew I had to immediately get back to work because it is through my work that I knew I could find the answer to my quest.

However, I also, knew that I must face the harrowing fact that there was Carol's funeral that must be attended to first. And, the pain I was feeling in my body would not compare to the pain that was coming with these arrangements.

Steve and Maddisen were heaven-sent in helping during this unbearable time of grief. While I was in the hospital, mostly in and out of consciousness and reality, they went through Carol's personal phone and called her parents.

Carol's parents and siblings were at the house when I got out of the hospital. I, not having any parents or close relatives, immediately clung to them as my immediate family – and they, too, embraced me. Together, we were able to comfort one another through our tears and love for the one that meant the world to each of us.

Grief is the most difficult of all emotions to deal with, and everyone has to deal with it themselves. I don't know if that is where the saying "misery loves company" comes from - but definitely, there is comfort in a hug or warm touch.

Chapter Three

The Trials

The police were very familiar with a predator by the nickname "Empty." He had a rap sheet a mile long and more than once been a suspect in a nationwide manhunt, the last resulting in his capture and a twenty year prison sentence.

You cannot tell if an animal is diseased just by looking at it. Likewise, you cannot tell if a human being is diseased or defective just by looking at them. But you can tell by their actions. Actions speak louder than words.

The authorities, once again, have "Empty" on their radar as a suspect in a series of break-ins and assaults around the Houston area. The break-ins quickly escalated to sexual assaults.

The assaults became more violent. These were usually committed against single women, or when the women were home alone. The police suspect that each incident was well planned. They were not just random assaults, but it is believed that there had been a reconnaissance of the intended victims with military precision. Each crime carried out with a planned precision.

Three weeks ago was the first incident in which a husband was involved. It is believed that with the precision of the first set of attacks, the fact the husband was home was no accident. The perpetrator had to add a new element to his game to keep it interesting and also a challenge. However, this new element could not pose a threat: it is only a pawn to be played to the gamer's advantage. It must only add and element of gamesmanship.

The husband had been tied up while his wife was raped then killed. He, too, was killed after his wife's killing. It is believed that the husband was aware of everything that was happening and did everything he could to free himself to go to the aid of his wife. This was evident by the injuries the husband sustained from the bindings. The injuries were evidence of quite a struggle to get free, which took a considerable amount of time to inflict, all to no avail. Apparently, to the perp, this added an element of enjoyment in knowing the husband was well aware of what was going on, and his horror raised the stakes of the game.

Then, a week ago, there was the second incident involving a husband. The crime scene was exactly the same as the previous incident involving a husband. There was only one exception: the perp did not kill the husband. The wife was assaulted then murdered. After a brutal sexual assault, the wife was stabbed numerous times with what appeared to be a hunting knife. The assault on his wife tormented the husband, and then he was badly beaten. However, the husband was allowed to live. He was able to identify the perpetrator as "M. T."

It now seems "Empty" has his "modus operandi" established. His new "M. O." is established and operational!

The police immediately knew they had a serial rapist and murderer on their hands. They also knew that this was not the last crime he would commit. They knew his past too well.

Empty's name and picture were plastered, 24 hours a day, in the media: television and newspaper, as well as, constant coverage on the radio. Within another 24 hours there were numerous reports of sightings. Roadblocks were set up for all traffic into and out of Houston. Another intense manhunt was under way.

My description of Carol's assailant confirmed "Empty" as the perpetrator. I now understood why it felt more like he was writing a name rather than initials on my forehead that horrible night. When he said his name was "Empty," the way he purposely said it, with a good Texas drawl, sounded like initials "M. T." Carol's

murder, along with the other recent crimes, caused the police to join forces with state and federal authorities for an all-out manhunt.

There were numerous reports of sightings across Houston immediately. Within two days the police had their suspect in custody.

Thinking he could hide in plain sight as just another homeless indigent was a big mistake on "Empty's" part. Just because they're homeless does not mean they belong to the same class of inhumanity as this animal, even if they wanted no part of him. One of the homeless men, who had been downtown trying to beg enough money for something to eat and, of course, a little wine for the stomach, saw his face on a news broadcast. He wanted no part of this kind in their surroundings. He immediately contacted the police and told them where the man they were hunting could be located.

The local, state, and federal law enforcement swarmed in with the force of an army. Now, Empty was no longer the predator. He, fittingly, became the victim. Only this time, the victim is not innocent. The stalking was precise, and the strike, with the power of a locomotive, was effective. Empty was singled out and captured before he knew what hit him. The police confirmed his nickname was "Empty." A handle his prison buddies had put on him because he had no feelings. They all said he was "empty" inside. So, he took the nickname of "Empty." He also took this as if he had just earned some sort of honorary degree. His real name is Robert Jones. Sounds so innocent!

Predators! The predator is a necessary element in the survival of life in a balanced animal kingdom. A diseased animal who becomes a diseased predator may be innocent and just a victim of a cruel twist of nature. A diseased human predator is no innocent victim: he only leaves in his path a trail of innocent victims!

Robert Jones first court appearance was Friday June 21, 2043 just one week after he brutally attacked and murdered Carol. Standing before the judge, Robert Jones was as "empty" of human emotions as he was last Friday when he brutally attacked Carol. If you were looking for a person who realized he had done wrong or gone too far, you were in the wrong courtroom! The only emotions this pathetic excuse for a human being displays are those of a wild beast; every contact becoming a

violent confrontation. Mr. Jones' arraignment is now his confrontation.

Once again a confrontation is about to take place. A predator has emerged. Only this is a confrontation between him and the territorial judge. Two warriors going head to head: the survival of the fittest. One defends the animalistic lust thrust upon the nearest available victim, and the other defends his territory. Let the battle begin!

Empty considered the judge to be another predator in the wild. This was his territory. He lived his whole life in the jungle. Tearing apart one predator after another was just a walk in the park for Empty, not to even mention the innocent just trying to survive in the wild.

But, this time, Empty was not in the wild. Not in the jungle. The rules have changed!

His trial and conviction should have been no difficult decision for anyone involved. The evidence gathered at the crime scenes was considered a "slam dunk" by the Prosecuting Attorney. However, getting the wheels of justice put into motion and turning to a final conclusion, I found, was not a simple process. Time was certainly not on our side.

Everything pointed to the guilt of this horrible monster, but it seemed every law on the books only protected him at every turn, and completely forgot about the victims, Carol being one of the most recent.

If you were a stranger sitting in the courtroom when the defense was presenting their case you, would think that Carol was the one that caused "this victim of circumstances" to commit this crime. He is just a victim of society who happened to land in this situation because society rejected him and cast him aside. To these people there is no such thing as bearing responsibility for your actions. No such thing as clear facts and evidence. To them everything is in a "gray area:" where right is wrong and wrong is right.

There were delays upon delays: inadmissible evidence, his rights, questionable witness: ad nauseam. All this just led to months upon months of waiting.

Over and over, I wondered, "Where was the protection and justice for Carol?"

Grieving for the loss of a member in the animal kingdom is expressed by each species in its own unique way. It is nature's built in mechanisms to mourn death. Death was not an element of the original creation but of disobedience. This mourning is also part of man's nature. Man can share in the morning. Man, also, has an element not found in the lower animal kingdom: hope.

After Carol's funeral, which is still too painful to talk about, and after my in-laws returned to Florida, I had a lot of time alone! Both my parents had passed. Mom to breast cancer at the early age of forty-two and Papa from a heart attack just two months after our wedding at the age of forty-eight. It looks like longevity does not run in my family. Sometimes, fate plays a cruel hand. Carol's parents are in their late sixties, as Carol was the oldest of six children. They are now retired in Miami. Longevity runs deep in her family.

There were many happy memories. Carol loved just the two of

us being together and doing simple things: the beach, biking, walking, or just sitting and talking over a hot cup of coffee or cappuccino. She also loved getting together with friends and talking and laughing until our jaws and sides ached. Carol loved living. Carol lived loving life and everything she came into contact with.

But, when the happy memories faded, there were also the dark times. The hard times! The nightmares! The scenes were playing over and over like a movie inside my head. Continually rewinding! Incessantly replaying the horror. I frantically searched, but there is no "STOP" button! I cry out for the words "THE END," but they never seem to appear. Only exhaustion brings relief when I am just too tired to even concentrate. Thinking is no longer possible!

Somehow, Empty knew what he was saying when he told me "I want to be sure that yours last a long, long time."

He had done this before and loved his game of horror. He loved the extreme immediate horror inflicted while he performed his animalistic acts on the wife. Always making sure the husband was positioned to view his home made movie projected on the bedroom walls. Empty knew it would be seared into the minds of the husbands he left behind for a lifetime of pain. He knew the mind had no "erase" button!

Then, there was the horror every time I looked in the mirror. Seeing the fresh scar on the side of my face immediately drove me back to that night. Maybe over time the scar will fade and the memory will heal as well.

I returned to work ten days after Carol's funeral. Being alone was the worst thing I could do. An idle mind is the devil's playground. And at this point, "Empty" was a personification of the devil. I was not going to give in to his game or his playground.

Getting back into a routine, I tried to convince myself that everything would turn out alright. I believed that our justice system, which had been around for over two hundred years, would prevail. I trusted in the "scales of justice." I also knew that today, the blindfold is being removed from the "Scales of Justice" as the judges legislate or promote their liberal agendas from the bench. And the individual being held accountable for his actions is becoming a thing of the past and society is now becoming the villain.

I also knew that I had made a promise to Carol. And I will fight to my last breath to keep that promise!

So, to keep me from going completely mad, I got together with Steve and had some deep discussions concerning my promise to Carol and my intentions to keep every last word of it. We talked, reasoned, and came up with some intriguing questions and answers.

We both were able to fill in the time between the actual court appearances caused by the delays of the lawyers trying to outdo one another with their courtroom pleonasm. These lawyers seem to enjoy their "minute in the spotlight" more than knowing that justice must be served. However, now, it was time to answer some of our "intriguing" questions. It was time to do something with our "intriguing" answers. It was time to put our thoughts into actions. Actions do speak louder than words!

There are no lingering repercussions to a predator's confrontation in the animal kingdom. Confrontations are handled and always end in defeat. Sometimes, the victor defeats the intruder for supremacy, and at other times, the defeat is in death of an opponent for life's sustenance.

Carol's parents and those of her siblings could attend almost every hearing and court date of the monster that killed Carol. After more than a year and a half the trial was finally making progress. We could see light at the end of the tunnel. By all projections it should be no more than two to three weeks until final arguments.

Steve and I were able to accomplish a lot these last eighteen months. Our plans have all been drawn up, and a pathway to success has been envisioned. "Carol. Hang in there. Things are looking up," I whispered. No one else could hear, but I knew Carol did.

These last three weeks have been intense. The anticipation! The fear! The hope! Every emotion one could imagine, all coming to a crescendo inside: exploding and riveting my whole body with emotional shrapnel. On one hand, there is great expectation, yet on the other, there is fear and uncertainty. Even if he is convicted, will it answer all the questions that have been crying out for answers from deep within my soul? Will this bring closure? Will this be the end of this nightmare? I hope so. But I fear not!

Repercussions are inherent to ones actions. There are lingering repercussions to a predator's confrontation! In the civilized world, we have a justice system to deal with these repercussions. It, too, sometimes ends in death.

All the witnesses have testified. All evidence has been presented. All the lawyers' games have been exhausted. Today is their final "Custer's Last Stand." Today, the lawyers were to present their final arguments.

Have you ever watch a rerun of Perry Mason on TV? How about some of the newer sophisticated "Lawyer" shows? That was all I could think about as I watched the battle at the front of the courtroom. Did these two think they were fighting for justice for what had happened to Carol? Or, were they auditioning for a role in what they thought was a surefire movie in the making?

I had this sickening feeling deep within. Not because I didn't think the jury would find Robert Jones guilty. It was because I was appalled at what our justice system had become as it tries to obtain a verdict.

Even after the brutality Carol suffered at the hands of the "accused" in her death, now, her memory and her spirit were once again being violated, and she had to suffer. Suffer at the verbal abuse of slimy lawyers, who, with insinuations against the victim, try to justify or dismiss the actions of their client in the name of "reasonable doubt."

Then there are the reporters who try the case in the court of public opinion. Trying to pretend they were just doing what was best to serve public interest as they go about trying to idolize the criminal and put a cloud of darkness over the victim.

Whether inside the halls of justice or outside in the court of public opinion, is there really such a thing as real justice anymore? Oh, yes, and of course, all within the law.

Real justice? Yes! We'll see! One day we all will stand before the real Judge and plead our case. Let's see how their "pleonasm" plays out in the Eternal Courtroom!

Things are very basic in the animal kingdom. It is set in stone. They live and die by the code. Man, too, has a code. A civilized society has "live and let live" codes ingrained: "Do unto others as you would have them do unto you." Man has also developed a system of justice to assure that obligation is maintained. This justice is for those who have been wronged. There also, is justice to those that have wronged others or society. Many live and die because of our system: its effectiveness or ineffectiveness. Is it perfect or is it flawed?

Justice? That is the "million dollar" question. That is the question that I intend to answer!

Chapter Four
The Verdict

Now, September 14, 2045, a little more than two years later, the verdict was finally due. The judge had called court back into session.

"Would everyone please rise? The court is now in session," the Bailiff cried out.

Those words brought the hope that this "nightmare" was finally over. It was a good thing Steve was there by my side, as he has been throughout this whole trial, because I was trembling from head to toe. Even with all the evidence, I was not one hundred percent sure they would convict him of first-degree murder, which is the only conviction that would give the death sentence. This monster had no right to live.

The predator knows that the prey must be terminated. Allowing the prey to continue to live means the survival of the fittest can be in jeopardy. Once the prey is put down, there is no further fear or threat.

The judge orders the jury in. There was a deafening silence over the courtroom as the jury filed in and took their seats. The judge asked, "Has the jury reached a verdict?"

Upon hearing this question, the Foreman of the jury stood and replied, "Yes, Your Honor, we have."

Then the judge said, "What say Ye?"

The Foreman unfolded a piece of paper he was holding and read it to the judge, "We the jury, find Robert Jones, guilty! Guilty of murder in the first degree."

Just as a prey who had been put down, allows survival, so too, once a predator is put down, humanity can rest at ease.

It was all I could do to remain quiet in my seat. I wanted to jump up and scream with all my might, "Yes, YES! Give the monster what's coming to him! Kill the Bastard the same way he killed Carol!" But I knew this was not something that I could do.

The judge then thanked the jury for their service and the attorneys for their work. He then thanked the participants and all the people who attended. Lastly, the judge stated, "The court will reconvene in 30 days for sentencing. Court dismissed."

Even at the end of the trial, it wasn't over. There was more waiting. More time for my own punishment: anticipating, wondering whether Robert Jones would be put to death. In the meanwhile, Robert Jones enjoyed the life he had spent most of his adult years living: in jail, tormenting other prisoners. He was allowed to continue playing his game!

****

Wednesday, Oct. 14, 2045, one long month after the verdict, came the sentencing portion of the trial. I just could not help anticipating this day. I have longed for it for over two years. The day this monster would be told he would die for what he did to Carol. I wanted him to experience the pain of death, just as Carol had experienced!

Once again, the court was called into session as the judge entered from a door to the right of the bench. "Everyone rise! The court is now in session," the Bailiff once again cried out. We had been here and performed this routine so many times it was an automatic reaction: when we saw the judge's chamber door starting to open everyone jumped to their feet. After the judge entered and sat down, we sat back down in our seats.

The judge began to speak. He spoke of the cruel punishment Robert Jones had inflicted, not only upon Carol, but the lingering pain that I, and others, would suffer the rest of our lives. He also told Robert Jones that he could not imagine any human being doing what he did to another unless he was totally devoid of emotion and had no feelings. "A person would have to be EMPTY of humanity to do what you did," the judge said, staring intently into the eyes of Robert Jones, observing to see if there were any signs of humanity. I don't believe he saw any.

I looked over at Robert Jones, and all I could see was a small grin on his face. Robert Jones looked as if he had just scored some sort of victory. The world now knew "Empty!" If it had not known before, the world was now being introduced to pure evil!

The judge then stated that within the confines of the law, no punishment would ever equal the punishment he had put his victims through. "So, Mr. Robert Jones, I hereby sentence you to die by lethal injection for the crimes you have committed. The court is adjourned."

There it is! It is finished! Robert Jones has been condemned to die. However, the administering of the courts sentencing would only take place after a long and lengthy appeals process. Hopefully, this sentence will be carried out, but with today's judicial system, there are no guarantees. The commute of this sentence is only a "Liberal" away.

As I was not allowed to show any response to the conviction or sentencing, I had to hold everything inside until it was all over and we left the courtroom. Walking down the courthouse steps, I could hold it in no longer. Angry at what I just heard I turned to Steve and said, "This man brutally raped and murdered Carol!

This man mocked me with the blood of Carol on his hands. He then did everything but kill me." My blood was way past the boiling point at this moment. Pounding my fists above my head in frustration I continued, "And now, this poor excuse for a human being is to be 'mercifully' administered a lethal dose so that his life will be 'peacefully' ended."

"That's our system." Steve said, and then continued, "That's our justice system."

I said, "You mean, he can violently, unmercifully take the life of an innocent individual, and we are duty bound to be most humane in administering to him his due punishment?"

Steve just looked at me as if to throw up his hands and say, "What do you want me to do? He got exactly what the law allows."

As we continued walking to our car I kept going over and over, in my mind, what Steve had said, "That's our system. That's our justice system."

The more I considered it, the more infuriated I became. "NO WAY!" I shouted! "That is pure B.S.", I continued.

What ever happened to real justice? You violently kill; you should equally have to pay. You brutally kill; you should brutally die! You unmercifully take the life of another; your life should be taken unmercifully. This is equal justice. This would be true capital punishment.

I said to Steve as we started to get in his car, "What ever happened to 'An eye for an eye'?" I did not expect an answer from him, but I just wanted to make my point.

Something must be done!

Silently, Steve drove me home. All the while, everything was churning in my head. Just as we entered the security gates into 'The Northsides,' it hit me. Empty's last words to me were, "An eye for an eye, man." No way is this piece of human dung going to peacefully lie there and dream off into "never, never land!"

As we pulled into my driveway, I leaned over to Steve and said, "I promised Carol, at her funeral, I would never let this monster get away with this." With tears streaming down my face, I turned to Steve, almost pleading for help, answers, and whatever, as I said, "I promised her and I will never let that happen."

There will be "an eye for and eye."

The prey is conquered. The predator is conquered. The kingdom and society are the overcomers.

Now, after our many discussions of these past two years, I can tell Steve what I think he can really do to help. I am going to need all the help I can get. I know I can count on Steve!

Chapter Five

The Problem

Crime and punishment in America is a joke. Each state has the right to make its own laws concerning this matter. However, once the laws are written and in some cases, passed by the voters, they are not necessarily the law of the land. The State or Federal Government has the right to step in by way of court actions to rule whether or not the laws meet within the guidelines of the Constitution. These laws are supposedly researched before being written, passed, or presented to the voters as to their Constitutionality. However, it is not always the Constitution that wins out but an agenda by the court, some of whom could care less about the Constitution, even when the case eventually ends up in the highest courts. Just look at what has happened and is still happening in State after State in our country.

I know, they, the ones writing the laws or sitting on the bench executing the law, don't get personally involved with what you and I experience due to the violent acts of criminal who brutally takes a life of your loved one or ones. The law does not deal with this horror; it only deals with the "black and white" letters of the law. How do we create laws that have empathy in them and still fulfill the letter of the law? That, too, is something that I must find out to fulfill my promise to Carol.

These justices, the Supreme Court Justices, in our states and in the Federal

Government, who are so highly trained and so duly authorized, can overturn any decision in the land issued by a lower court judge, jury or groups of citizens; yes even a state's constitutional amendment. These men and women can even overturn the vote of an entire state and maybe even the entire nation. So, it is no wonder that punishment does not work as a deterrent against crime. In the case of capital punishment, by the time the courts get through striking down one another, it can take ten to twenty years, if at all, to administer the punishment handed down by a judge.

My first task is to work to get this justice system changed and back on track. "We the people" have every right to all the protections a civil society is responsible to provide their people. Some may have a different desire or idea as to what that responsibility is concerning our system of justice and the effect it has on those who violate it. But more importantly, what effect it has on those who have been violated! But it is very clear that this inherent right of protection is not how our system of justice is working today!

This fact is well proven by the number of criminals on the streets today, who have been in and out of the system, as if our justice system were a department store with a revolving door and they just dropped by for a quick sale item. Most of these may be petty criminals, but at some point, a circumstance or situation, in the act of committing their crime, may cause an escalation into violence or even become life-threatening. Just consider the case in Florida where an innocent "neighborhood watch" turned deadly.

Yes, prisons are overcrowded. They try to make you believe it's because of the "good" justice system, but in reality, many are there as repeat offenders who were not dealt with properly the first, second or even the third time and are still caught in the "revolving door." Others are there because our current system is much like "welfare." They cannot survive on the outside on their own. The prison gives them what every innocent person works hard for every day: a roof over their head, food, clothing, entertainment and security. These people, the criminal element in our society, are not there because they worked hard for these benefits but because they denied someone who worked for these benefits. The criminal then stole, destroyed, disabled, or prevented the person from having these benefits. The prison population is not the defining factor of a good justice system!

What would be a good factor to define our justice system? Would it not be that a predator, who is out to satisfy selfish lust or desire, is dealt justly and harshly according to the law as it should be intended to correct the evil against society?

Our current system of justice places criminals into three basic categories:

1. Petty criminals: Administrative Infractions, Regulatory Offenses, and Misdemeanors – punishable with less than one year in jail (usually a local jail), restitution, etc.
2. Felony: Assault, Embezzlement, Robbery, Kidnapping, etc. – punishable with one year or more in prison plus judge's discretion.
3. Capital Offense: Murder, Manslaughter, Mayhem, etc. – punishable with 10 years to life in prison or the death penalty.

My concern is mainly with the third category. These are the hardcore who commit the most violent of crimes: revenge, murder and mayhem. No matter what category they're in, all must be dealt with properly, and proper punishment must be administered as a deterrent.

But, in today's system, criminals with their high-profile lawyers are allowed to play the system until justice for the victims seems beyond reach.

In the animal kingdom, the predator has very little need for a court to intervene. However, when the brood or head leader feels the rules of the pact has been violated, he will be sure justice in the name of the pact is upheld quickly, by whatever means the pact requires.

We, the victims, sit in the courts, watching and waiting for quick justice, all the while having to replay the horrors of the event over and over, once again suffering as if it has just happened: enduring the same pains, not physically, but the excruciating horror and grief. These people, who are charged with seeing that justice is done, deny the victims peace as they drag out the trials with whatever delays they can conjure up to produce before the court.

Again, the first thing I will do is set my focus on this last category, "the hardcore," the ones, whom I am most concerned about: although a system will be developed to deal with all levels of crime, in the hopes that they will be deterred from escalating to the "hardcore" category. The hardcore are the ones who prey like animals on the innocent to fulfill their lust and evil desires: those whom I consider inhuman. This is the element that the justice system has failed to deter the most!

Chapter Six

The Task

I must work to create a wave across America of voter rights and authority. We have the RIGHT, as Americans - we are a Democratic Republic - to elect the proper individuals to represent us and to create laws that protect us and guarantee that not only our rights are upheld but that the horrors created by these type of predators are eliminated. And if this is not the case, we have the right to lobby against unfair laws and to change those representatives who do not adequately represent us. This includes any person, department or official elected or appointed! As the people whom our forefather envisioned in charge of running this country, we must diligently scrutinize every person's performance in our government to be sure they are doing their job and not overstepping the enumerated duties, responsibilities, and privilege of their position.

This, as citizens of this great Country, must be our fight to protect not only property and life but protect against the "horror" that many of these crimes inflict on not only the victim but on many of their loved ones. Because, grieving is a factor associated with many hardcore crimes and, in some cases, may last a life time, while the predator is being carefully treated so as not to infringe upon his "constitutional rights!"

Therefore, within the Constitution's provisions, it is a MUST that we have a uniform bill for punishment, on a national level, for all crimes, whether minor or a capital offense, doing away with the inequities between the states. Therefore, it would be justified, that all crimes fall under Federal jurisdiction and all punishment of these offenses are administered at a Federal level.

****

We spent the next ten months getting petitions signed in every state. We also had to spend and enormous amount of time on fund raising for an effective media campaign. Our initiative is for a Constitutional Amendment for a national crime bill. This bill will reform how and by whom crime and punishment are handled, removing all jurisdictions from the states. Therefore, under a Constitutional Amendment all crime and punishment will fall under Federal jurisdiction. This amendment is the Punishment and Enforcement Systems Act (PESA).

I have spent four long years playing the political game, a game that is just as bad and corrupt as the legal system. Four years of public and private appearances, lobbying, and brown-nosing to get something done, which should only require a couple minutes to ask about and sign the papers. But, No! Not in this country of politicians where everyone is looking for what benefit they will get, even for doing the right thing. They are looking for the one big news-grabbing gimmick to vault them to the top of their party.

To get something worthwhile done you have to kiss the ass of everyone in Washington or get run out of town without even a "goodbye." Fine, so I had to kiss a lot of asses: which not only spoke of my actions but the character of those I had to deal with.

Four long years, having to set aside dealing with my own grief to try and educate the system, that what justice alone cannot accomplice it must also help in the healing process of the victims.

Finally, after much time and politicking and with the aid of many groups backing me, not all of which I am proud to be associated with, we will be on the ballot in the next General Election, November 2052: we were too late for the mid-term 2050 election. After all is said and done and we have won, we will see who kisses what!

I had considered developing a system as soon as the trial was over and started immediately working with Steve on a solution. We worked on this task even while we were politicking to get this bill written for a Constitutional Amendment.

Chapter Seven

Researching the Problem

While waiting for the 2052 election to get a Constitutional Amendment dealing with crime and punishment and as the major proponent of the PESA bill, which I developed and fought four hard, long years for, I had been assigned the task to design and develop a punishment system that would be fair, equal, and produce a crime deterrent to all offenders

Certain questions must be explored and answered before any system of correction can be developed. Concerning crime, we must ask "Where, When, Why, and How." These are appropriate questions that must be answered before the development of a proper functioning system.

WHERE does crime exist? Of the four questions this is the easiest of all to answer. EVERYWHERE!

WHEN does crime exist? Again, this is a fairly simple one to answer. Anytime someone commits an unlawful act that is against a civilized society or a member of such society, it is a crime!

WHY does crime exist? Crime exists because there are people who commit unacceptable acts against society. Which begs to answer the question, why do criminals exist? Criminals exist because there are those among us who do not adhere to the rules of God, society, or nature. Crime and criminals are one.

HOW does crime exist? This is the crux of the matter. The other three questions rest alone on the determination of this answer, yet the juxtaposition of how is a sum total or a combination of the other three questions. And all are answered by one word: tolerance! We have become a society that is so politically correct that we are tolerant of unsociable behavior. We have become tolerant to the extent that we allow for correction as long as it doesn't go against our moral, social, political, or religious beliefs. Just look at the many protest at capital punishment of someone who has committed a brutal or multiple murders. Until we no longer allow the "where, when, and why" the "how" will continue to exist. But, when we no longer allow the "how" the "where, why, and when" will also no longer exist. Crime can and must be contained and eventually done away with!

Again, why does crime i.e.: criminals exist? How do the answers to the "where, when, why, and how" become manageable elements to help control and or eradicate crime? Did something go wrong in their growth process or was their basic human life at birth defective? These, too, were major questions that had to be answered in order to develop a Moral Understanding Sensory and Control (MUSaC) unit. This unit would be the controlling element of any deterrent or punishment system. MUSaC would be built as the controlling element of any device that would become functional to meet the Punishment and Enforcement Systems Act (PESA) guidelines, to be voted on in 2052. If this amendment is passed, a functioning system must be ready for use within twelve months of the passing of the bill by the voters, or it will become null and void.

Are we all born equal? The Declaration of Independence states that we are: 'We hold these truths to be self-evident, that all men are created equal, that their Creator endows them with certain 'Unalienable Rights' that among these are 'Life, Liberty and the pursuit of Happiness'."

Life is also in question as the abortion issue is almost tearing this country apart. Even those elected officials, sworn to protect "Life, Liberty and the Pursuit of Happiness," have failed us many times and especial in the matter of life. Their voting, back in 2025, to not even protect a baby born alive during an abortion with life-saving medical attention is an enormous failure to protect "Life!" Liberty, too, is on the chopping block as an oppressive government tries to do away with many of our rights. Happiness is challenged many times by the horrors that produce grieving to the core due to the predator and his vicious crimes: who, many times, are put back on the streets to strike again and again.

However, not all circumstances, opportunities, or abilities are equal; some due to birth others due to circumstances: location, economics, inheritance or natural process. We are all born with the basics of human life: a body, a brain, a soul and a spirit. In these traits, we are created equal, except for those with disabilities who, for some unknown reason or a cruel twist of fate, are lacking in some respect in one of these areas. However, we are all still equal in our God-given rights! Neither man nor government can give nor take away these rights!

A body must be fed nutrients through the intake of a somewhat healthy diet. We have been instilled with basic survival skills (walking, talking, hygiene, etc.) to grow up into a healthy, mature adult. Without the proper care and nourishment there is atrophy.

The brain must be fed information (parental training, formal education, basic experiences gained in society, etc.). Without the proper input of information, there is impedance.

The soul must be taught its proper responses to its emotions (desires, lust, love, hate, relationships, etc.), its mind (the thought and reasoning process), and its will (the decision process of when to be aggressive, submissive, or neutral and when to act upon them). Without the proper social and spiritual input one becomes anathema.

And lastly, the spirit (conscience, intuition and fellowship) must be exercised to be strengthened. We must learn to listen to our conscience (learning right from wrong, what the proper behavior is and what is not, etc.). We must learn to become sensitive to its intuition (to know when to act and when to beware). Lastly, and probably the most important of all, we must not neglect its fellowship (this is the spiritual part when man communicates with his Creator, which also gives guidance to the conscience and intuition).

Basically, having the same start, we all must mature and grow each of these attributes into solid, mature human beings. Otherwise, we become "defective humans" in a civil society. And, defective humans eventually produce a defective society!

Chapter Eight
Developing a System

The government required much research concerning the issues and problems of such an undertaking. I was able, after many sleepless nights, to keep up with this research while I was lobbying Congress and playing their political game. Now that the required research and the political game playing are finished, it is time to build the product (which I have a little secret that only Steve and I are aware of and soon to be revealed).

After much thought concerning the issues and problems and what is needed to deal with them, I came to only one conclusion: human beings have been unable to cope with the problem. I am also sure of this one thing - Robotics cannot deal with the problem because humans control them: whether it is because of their changing ethics or their unwillingness – I am not sure. Robotics will not be capable because they cannot act on their own, independently of human input. The only conclusion: there must be a merging of the two to produce a new element that, once developed, cannot be changed, influenced, or controlled by humans.

After much thought and deliberations, Steve and I decided that the cloning of a human with a robot is the answer. A **CLOBOT**. A **CLO**ned-ro**BOT**.

A CloBot is a robotic replica of a

human being physically capable of containing human characteristics: walking, talking, etc. It will also be able to have functioning capabilities through the input of DNA and DNA characteristic programming: acting, reasoning, thinking, performing. These robots will then become cloned human beings.

CloBots will be made with neutral DNA: they are gender neutral, no soul, no self, no spirit, and no character. All human fundamentals will be the results of the input of DNA obtained from humans at the time of assignment. Before input, you have a virtual human being with a brain, which can calculate body needs and functions and supply necessary commands to sustain life without human interaction. A CloBot, without DNA has no character and cannot relate to others: there is no social interaction (good or bad). DNA is the activating element in order to perform and function as a human. It is like a car with its motor running but the transmission is in neutral.

With the advantage of working in the Deep Space Habitation and Exploration department at WOSE, I am very proficient in developing Robotic Apparatuses. Plus, I also have the expertise of Steve, my best friend, who has hung right by my side through all of this and has a few more years at WOSE than I. Steve was more than happy to assist me and make his knowledge and skills available. It is time to get into the trenches!

With our job experiences in robotics and the use of the most sophisticated computers in the world, we have been secretly working and applying our knowledge on a system with just the day in mind that an "Eye for an Eye" capital punishment system would be accepted. Steve and I have worked tirelessly these past years, even as we were getting the political and social measures passed. We have developed a system that is "fair." We have a system that is "equal." And, most of all, we have a system that will be a "crime deterrent" as well as a capital punishment system. With the end goal in mind and working carefully within the constraints of the Constitutional Amendment, our system only needs tweaked to meet what I am sure will be the government's approval. We have worked relentlessly on this project and now it will be finished and ready by the time voting is done. Now, our secret has been revealed!

Chapter Nine

The System

Science has come a long way since the beginning of the space program, especially in the field of Robotics. I'm sure the world would be shocked, as well as amazed, if they only knew just how far science has progressed. The combing of man and machine has now become a reality in our secret project. Through the merging of genetic research, which is more Steve's department, and advancement of computerized robots, which is my department, we have made man and machine one. The CloBot: a human robot.

Through Clobonics (Gene duplication of man with Robots), we

can reproduce or clone any human being, dead or alive, in a matter minutes. This is possible as long as we can obtain a sample of blood, hair, tissue, or other trace evidence. Our new built in DNA extractor system can extract DNA from a viable sample and have a usable profile ready for sensitizing the unit in a matter of minutes.

Why do you think there have been numerous sightings of such dead personalities as Elvis, JFK, and Epstein over these past few years? Or, even Big Foot, as we were testing the limits, along with having some fun. Answer: the testing program of our Humanic Research. We have perfected the process. Now, for its ultimate purpose - to rid the world of crime!

The system is called "Clobonic

Administered Punishment Systems (CAPS)." This system will be the enforcing mechanism of the Punishment and Enforcement Systems Act (PESA) and will be administered using two different methods:

Method A: The CloBot Termination Device (CTD): or as Steve and I like to call it RX: Robotic Executioner.

Method B: The CloBotic Correctional Implant Device (CCID).

There is a specific purpose and use for each device, which I fully explain below:

Device A - The CloBot Termination Device (CTD): is for those who commit Capital Punishment crimes and are sentenced to death. The CTD will administer punishment in the manner the crime was committed. The death portion will be unrestricted, but other acts committed during the crime, such as rape will not be repeated, only the magnitude of the act: mental anguish, fear, horror, etc. The CloBot Termination Device is a simulated human programmed to inflict termination (capital punishment, death).

When manufactured, the CloBot is programmed with a neutral moral coding: it does not distinguish "good from bad" or "right from wrong," until the input of DNA. However, when sensitized with the perpetrator's DNA, along with the DNA programming, the neutral moral coding becomes altered with the same moral concepts and actions of the perp. It is now programmed to act and execute in the same manner performed in the original acts.

After completing its mission of administering retribution, the CloBot will be desensitized. It will be neutralized by the removal of DNA and DNA programming from the CPU, which triggers action. It will also be de-morphed by the removal of DNA from the morphing unit, causing the unit to return to its neutral generic animation state. The unit is then stored for future use. Upon neutralization the unit will return to its original state of neutrality and will not be a functional until it is once again induced with DNA.

Device B - The CloBotic Correctional Implant Device (CCID): this device is not a simulated human, as that of the CTD. The CCID is a very small device with programming functions based on the software in the CTD. It is the size of a mini-microchip. This device is for the immediate correction and prevention of future crimes by a convicted criminal.

For those that commit lesser crimes (Administrative Infractions, Misdemeanors, etc.) that are not punishable by death, the CloBotic Correctional Implant Device will not be used until repeated offenses. It will then be at the judge's discretion when to order its use, becoming mandatory after the fifth offense. However, it is believed that the threat of the implant will in itself become a deterrent. The CCID will be used for both:

Felony: One Offense, Assault, Embezzlement, Robbery, Burglary, etc.

Felony: Two Offenses, Kidnapping, Armed Robbery, Drug Distribution, etc.

This implant will not have any DNA but only a Predesigned Moral Correctional Code (PMCC). The implant is small, using an embedded program that will not stop the person from having criminal thoughts but, will stop him from acting on them through behavioral corrections.

The implant is to be implanted into the SOUL of the human being. Most everyone, at one time or another, has had or will have this feeling in the chest that your heart is being ripped out or a strong emotional feeling when your heart seems to flutter. These feeling may be in response to the death of a dear loved one, serious injury to a child, a proud parent attending the graduation of their son or daughter, or a number of other things. This is not the actions of our physical heart, but these feelings are in the exact same place. The physical heart is nothing more than a blood pump. It does not produce feelings of sorrow, happiness, love, hate and so on. These feelings reside in what is known as our soul.

The soul consists of your mind (not to be confused with your brain), your emotions, and your will. We all have sensations that resonate within our body from these three parts of our soul. What was thought to be attributes, until recently have been found to exist as a member of our body: the soul. Research has finally located the soul, and it surrounds the heart: that is why the feelings are in the location of the area of our heart. No, a surgeon cannot open you up and take it out, and show it to everyone. It is invisible, just like our breath. Our thoughts, feelings, and decisions are also invisible: being invisible does not negate the fact that they are part of our being. Our soul is an organ just as much as our spirit, which is also invisible. And, when it is engaged, the feelings are in the same place in the body in everyone. We now know where it exists and, therefore, can implant the CCID into it. This device will then control the criminal actions that a corrupted soul demands. Part of this control is to initiate a moral behavioral treatment and adjustment program from within.

The CCID is for those who have reached court-mandated implantation of a behavioral correctional unit: the CCID. This device will be infused with the spirit of morality (Good), and will be a required implantation into the soul of those who commit crimes which require this implant for correction.

My research has found that it is in the soul that crime is carried out. I have found that it starts in either the mind (thought process) or in the desires (emotions) and is engaged (carried out) by the will. This implantation device, CCID, will impact a person every moment, day and night, to guard, expose, and correct any criminal (Evil) behavior.

The person may still think about committing a crime or the desire to commit a crime. However, the CCID deals with actions, and with the programming intervention, they will be unable to act out the crime: their will cannot put these thoughts or desires into motion. The CCID will use its programming for correction and rehabilitation. It stops them, forcing them to reconsider their actions and make a choice to do what is right.

The implant will remain functioning until a complete rehabilitation is effected: predetermined sensory programming will determine when, or if, the desired effect of rehabilitation has been achieved, and the individual will be referred to the National Moral Review Board (NMRB). The board then will determine if regeneration has been completed and order the neutralization of the implant. Once implanted, the implant remains for life and can be re-activated.

Now we wait. Now is the time for "we the people" to take our country back from the criminals!

Chapter Ten
Criminals Beware

The election is over, and our capital punishment reform act has passed with an overwhelming majority. I feel that we are on track to reveal the new system within the next month. I believe also that the election of a new President, who has pushed for this reform from the beginning of his campaign, will also be a great help in the implementing of this system in a much smoother, quicker manner: although, I am sure there will be court challenges as to the Constitutionality of the amendment.

The first Capital Punishment Center is to be built in Los Angeles.

Los Angeles was chosen mainly because of the major movie studios, which will be accessed in set design. The second center is scheduled for New York and others to follow throughout the country. All details will be revealed at the Los Angeles center groundbreaking ceremony the first Friday of January, which is January 8, 2053, just over two months away.

Fridays are usually the best day for ceremonies. It's the end of the week, and no one wants to work. Everyone will still be recovering from the Christmas and New Year's holiday festivities. If everyone is like me, it takes quite a while to get back into the rhythm of working after the holidays, especially for those of us who use vacation time to take an extended time of celebrating between Christmas and New Year's.

The Governor, Mayor, many big shots from the movie studios, the Press, law enforcement, and many from the general public will be present. Hopefully, this will turn out to be one big unveiling event. Everyone seems to be talking optimistically, in private, the pre-press, and publicly, expressing their hope that crime could now be controlled. All will be there to get the first glimpse of this new device, whatever it is, that is supposed to clean up America and maybe the whole world.

America, this is where we once lived with our doors unlocked and walking our neighborhood streets at night. Now, we must put up iron bars on the door and windows, and we can't even stick our heads out after dark because of the drive-by shootings. Crime today is much worse than I ever thought it would get, looking back more than five years ago when I started this project. Now, they predict that five out of every six children will be a victim of a violent crime at some point in their lives.

But, all of that is about to change: criminals beware!

Chapter Eleven

The Introduction

I stepped to the microphone, and said,

"Well, today, January 08, 2053, is finally here, it is a new day! Crime and criminals beware! This is the day you will now get your first glimpse of the future. A future where crime and its perpetrators better be on guard." Steve stood next to me with one hand on one side of the cloth covering the Clobot and I had the other side. I continued by saying,

"We now have a future that not only will curb crime but one day eradicates it all together." As I said this, Steve and I yanked the cloth, covering the Clobot, as I continued speaking,

"Behold the future!" With the unveiling of the Clobot, I said,

"Meet 'RX' the Robotic Executioner." "RX" is the nickname Steve and I gave the robot as we personally got to know it. RX manufacturing was complete on December 12, 2052 and the first CloBot was assigned production number A141212OU001. That gave us a little over a month to run it through its trials and be sure there were no kinks. Everything seemed to be in working order with only a few minor tweaks. We are ready to go!

The Governor stepped to the microphone and the ceremonies began.

He boldly declared, "Today is the beginning of a new era in crime fighting and prevention. Unlike the days of Wyatt Earp, Elliott Ness and J. Edgar Hoover, today you will see a crime fighter that will not just fight against crime but will send a new message to the criminals." The Governor went on for about thirty minutes giving facts and figures concerning today's crime epidemic. "Well," he said, "We are tired and we are not going to take it anymore! Behold, the future!" he said as he turned and gave a big thumbs up as he pointed to the future crime fighter.

You can never anticipate what a crowd may or may not expect at a gathering such as this. Because of the pre-press hype, I wondered if expectations were too high, too low, or ….? So, I decided, let's just find out. At the unveiling, most sat there still somewhat puzzled. There before them stood what appeared to be perhaps the most beautiful woman they have ever seen? Yes, with my first CloBot production, standing before them was Carol!

It was only fitting the first likeness and the first implementing of RX should be Carol for she is the reason this whole program came into being.

Yes, it was very difficult to stand there and look at her. Every emotion in my body welled up as I had to stop and make myself realize that it was not Carol. The likeness was so real I just wanted to reach out and touch her just one more time. You think you have gotten hold of yourself and that you can handle it but in a moment everything is just as it was that night. There is never an end to it; once you've lived a nightmare, it's always there to come roaring back, again and again. Having lost your wife is the loneliest existence a man can feel.

I knew at this point I must get a hold of myself as I was being introduced as the originator and designer of this project who would explain its use and application, which I did at length.

The Governor finished his speech and introduced the Mayor who also gave words of encouragement, for they both had dealt with crime on every level of their life as servants of the people. After the Mayor finish he turned the microphone back over to me.

I asked for a volunteer to donate a little blood for our demonstration, as blood works quicker because of its all inherent properties. Most were hesitant but one brave reporter, John Smitty, stepped forward. A paramedic approached him and assured him everything was alright and he wouldn't feel a thing. The paramedic withdrew the blood and injected it into one of Carol's....I mean RX's injection ports. I then explained that when a crime is committed, and a person is convicted and sentenced to death as punishment for that crime, RX would be the means of execution.

There are other features of RX that I did not go into at the beginning but would explain before the presentation concluded.

I went on to explain to the crowd, "Everyone wants justice done. And from the days of old, justice was equated with an "eye for an eye." This is today's motto for our newly passed federal Capital Punishment System, "An Eye for an Eye!"

After letting that information sink in for a few seconds I continued, "Having been convicted and sentenced to death, details from court transcripts concerning the nature of the crime and its setting will be given to the movie studios to be re-created in every detail. This same information will be fed into the programming apparatus of the

CloBot, who will become the actual perpetrator of the crime. The original perpetrator will now become the victim. This is the function of RX, the Robotic Executioner! The act of being put to death by an RX is known as RX-ecution (pronounced Rex-e-cution). As the actual victim's revenge will be realized upon the perpetrator."

How is the victim's revenge accomplished? RX actually has two injection ports. One is for identity purposes only (the taking on of a complete outward appearance of the person). This is to be used to quickly identify a person who has committed a crime or to give RX the outward appearance of the victim of the capital punishment crime when performing an execution. The second port is for a complete inner duplication of actions of the criminal so that RX can duplicate the same execution on the criminal.

Trying to break the tension, I asked, "Why the movie studios?" Giving a little more time for everyone to relax before I answered I reached for a bottle of water and took a long drink before continuing, "Each case will be made into a docudrama, and the proceeds will go to the families of the victim(s). The showing of these docudramas will also spread the word to the criminals that we are coming for you and this is what you have to look forward to!"

As they were listening to me I knew I did not have their full attention.. Many were being distracted by what was happening to RX, whom I was standing next to. This lovely woman was being transformed into a man. It seemed to be some sort of metabolic physical change. No one was touching it or restructuring it. There were no wires attached, yet a new person was evolving. It was almost getting difficult to speak over the murmur of the crowd, at this point, as everyone had turned to look and see that it was no longer the beautiful voluptuous body of Carol. What they saw, just in these few minutes since the injection was that there were muscles becoming developed and hair was beginning to grow on its arms, chest and legs. Also, masculine facial features and hair began to form.

The crowd became more and more intrigued as they realized that right before their very eyes a human being, the brave young press reporter, John

Smitty, was being duplicated. Everything was to be duplicated down to the minutest detail: except for genitalia which is not used in the administration of punishment.

As the "Humanic" process continued I went on to explain how a person convicted of a crime would be punished in the same manner their own victim had been. The people began to believe and this brought a standing ovation, maybe not to what I said because I'm not sure how many were listening at this point. "At last, an eye for an eye," someone shouted.

As the duplication process continued, I went on to explain that not only is this a capital punishment system, but one of the greatest crime deterrents ever! Now is the time to reveal other features and benefits of the

Clobots. I told them that now we can take evidence from a crime scene and with the discovery of any hair, blood or tissue of the perpetrator we can reproduce them not only in looks but in psyche. Their face will then be displayed all across the country and they will have nowhere to hide. It will make the apprehension of criminals almost immediate before they have time to strike again. Can you imagine that every citizen will be aware of this criminal and on the lookout for them within minutes of the discovery of this trace evidence? There will also be a reward system set up to every citizen who cooperates in the apprehension of these criminals.

I finally finished my speaking and turned the microphone back to the Governor who then said there would now be a period for questions and answers.

Many of the questions were even directed to RX, whom they readily accepted as one of them, and were amazed to find its answers were no different than those of John Smitty's, from whom, he was cloned.

Chapter Twelve

The Tour

The next step was to give RX wide spread media coverage so that everyone will be familiar with him and what he will be doing. This will also put all those on guard that live and prey upon others that this will no longer be accepted or tolerated.

We also plan a campaign across the country, just like a politician running for office. We will have a campaign where the people can get a "hands on" feeling of what this program is all about and what it can do for them personally. They will also be able to see and feel a real CloBot, along with watching the metabolic physical change when induced.

We plan a "walk the streets of America" type of campaign so we can draw the people out and to assure every American that they no longer need to be afraid to walk the street day or night. That they no longer need to be afraid to leave their doors and windows unlocked. We plan to assure America that they no longer have to FEAR!

This is our country! We have the right to move about in it freely without the fear that has gripped this country for the past number of decades because of the terrible, senseless crime. RX will re-assure us that all will be well.

****

Our schedule for the next six months, or so, is to crisscross the country, covering every state from California to Main and from Texas to the Dakotas. Everywhere we have been so far the people have come out to see us in massive numbers. These are some of the largest crowds ever seen, no matter who or what the previous event held. Every stadium, park, convention center, and every other place a showing was made the place has been packed to overflowing. The kids seem to be the most excited of all. RX even seems to sense the presence of the children and has a special connection with them. Everyone just wants to touch him, like he was some sort of god or something. You can just feel the hope in the air from everyone in the crowds that this would all be true. That RX would truly be able to rid us of the scourge of the crime that has taken over our country today, and it would get rid of the fear permeating this country. That it would rid us of the senseless taking and the killing of our children, rid us of the brutal rape and murder of our young women. Rid us of the violent, senseless hate and killing between the gangs and the murder of the innocent bystanders who are gunned down because they are in the wrong place or even the right place at the wrong time. Yes, you can feel the hope and the anticipation. The hope that this would all be brought to an end by this special "person" they are seeing and touching, "RX." The anticipation, that it would soon become a reality!

Chapter Thirteen

The Implant

The new justice system is working well. The courts have been following the established guidelines for sentencing. When someone is convicted of a crime there is no doubt of their guilt since the CloBot is able to identify the perpetrator using the morphing unit. Now, sentencing is carried out immediately because there is no appeal process since there is no doubt of guilt. There have been a large number already receiving the implant device (CCID). There also have been some capital offenses where the termination device (CTD) has been ordered. These sentences will be carried out on a timely manner once the CloBots start arriving.

Carlos Alvaresario was the first to receive the implant device April 13, 2053. He is a repeat drug offender and dealer. If you met him on the streets or in a social setting you would think he was the nicest guy in the world. Carlos is like the brother you never had: intelligent, happy-go-lucky, and ready to talk about any subject: movies, sport, or politics, and probably anything else you could think of. But, Carlos had another side, a real troubling side: to him and to others.

Carlos was raised in a low-income family with eight siblings. Both his parents struggled to provide for Carlos and the kids: working many hours for very low wages. They loved their children and tried to give them a proper education and home life. However, Carlos learned at an early age to play the system, just as he learned to play his parents. He took to the streets at an early age because he thought he found more comfort with his street friends, who were nothing but thugs doing drugs and break-ins, than with the family who cared for him.

It wasn't long before Carlos, at the age of 13 had his first arrest. He was caught stealing from a local drug store. Carlos' excuse was, "I needed cigarettes! They had them, I didn't."

Carlos was release to his broken hearted parents. They tried talking to him and he agreed that it was stupid and that he will never do it again. Carlos played "the game" well.

Soon, his petty theft escalated to break-ins. He quickly learned that there was money to be made with the loot and that sure beat working. The break-ins became more frequent until Carlos had a pretty good stash of money, which he gave some to his parents, telling them he either won it playing basketball or found it.

Carlos was arrested the second time for "Breaking and Entering" and received the mandatory prison sentence of one year at the ripe old age of 14 years 4 months. He was sent to a youth detention center and again played the system and was released one year to the day with good behavior.

Back on the streets again it wasn't long before he was approached by one of his buddies about turning from that petty stuff to where the real money was: to turn that "little bit of money" into "big bucks." Carlos was all ears.

Carlos did not feel his selling drugs was all that bad as long as it wasn't sold to little kids and that he wasn't doing drugs himself. The "big bucks" came rather quickly. So, too, did the sampling of the wares!

Carlos was hooked by age 16. Now, the "big bucks" were also supporting a hefty personal habit for his personal use: and including the use for whatever girl was in his life at the time.

Carlos was very careful the first year of dealing. He made sure of all contacts and that they were known to or by the gang. However, like all that play this game, Carlos, made a mistake. He had no idea Julio Jemenez a confirmed buyer, was a Narc. Carlos was arrested for drug possession and distribution. Carlos was given the mandatory of three years or the choice of the implant. This judge was more progressive to get crime under control and instead of waiting for the third offense to order the implant he offered it after the second offense. The specifics of the implant were explained very clearly, as well as, the life behind bars: which Carlos was on a fast track to obtain. Most were happy to take the implant verses three years behind bars in a hard-core prison. Carlos did not hesitate,

"I want the implant!"

Carlos thought this sentencing was a "piece of cake" and he could go on living life as usual. No hard time for him!

It wasn't long until Carlos and his buddies got together and planned a sure fire break-in that "word had it" was worth a small fortune. Plans were made and set for tomorrow night, for they knew the owners were gone for the weekend. Carlos sure loved the new Justice System.

Carlos was the first and Candice "Candy" Callahamer was the second. Candy, too, had a drug problem but was arrested for embezzlement.

Candy worked for a large banking firm on Wall Street. She rose from receptionist to an account broker in record time. Candy was very smart and at first took night courses, studying hard to better herself.

But, like so many, the quick rise to prestige had its price. Her job required personal contact with many influential well to do people: especially men in the corporate world. These men liked to party!

Candy was a very attractive redhead. Five foot-five with a waist most women would die for, and Candy knew how to use her merchandises to work a party. This is a dangerous game to play. Candice Callahamer soon became familiar with these dangers.

Alcohol, a given, to be part of the game. However, many involved in the game had new elements to introduce to the players: sometimes unbeknownst to the recipient. That is what happened in Candy's case. She was slipped what is known as a "Mickey!"

Candy did not remember very much from the night before, but was told by others that called checking on her, that she really seemed to be having a good time last night: great, and not even a hangover.

The second time she was approached by the guy who slipped her the "Mickey," a guy that she had seen and partied with several times: "good looking," Bud Harrelsin. Only, this time he was very open about what happened last time and offered her some "Po Coke" so she could get the party on and bring back that "good feeling." Candy was very hesitant and said no. But, like most pushers Buddy boy was not about to give up.

The party life, even though a certain amount was required by her job, went far beyond what was required.

This life can become very addicting: a form of a drug in itself.

Buddy boy Bud was at almost every party. He was much more experienced than Candy and knew how to set a novice up. It wasn't long before Candy gave in and became hooked on the drugs he provided. It then became a necessary part of the party life.

It wasn't long after the drugs became a necessary part of her life that Candy had to come up with the cash if she wanted the stuff. That "good feeling party life" was no longer free. Candy had to find a way to pay for what had now become an expensive habit. Her salary, even though it was enough to have a very comfortable existence, was not close to supporting her habit.

Candy soon found her cash source. At first, she would only scam small amounts. I am no Bernie Madoff she thought to herself. These people I am scamming out of a little of their money won't even miss it. These were the high rollers she was scamming. Pocket change.

It wasn't long before flags started showing up in her dealings. Candy was confronted and denied everything. It wasn't long before she didn't have a leg to stand on as the evidence became more and more clear.

Candy Callahamer was arrested, convicted and sentenced to five years in prison. With five years being a major amount of time in one's life, Candy was given the choice between the original sentence or the CCID. Just as so many others have done, when given the choice, Candy chose the CCID.

The courts are happy when one makes this choice because they know that person will not be part of the revolving door and will not appear before them again. They will be rehabilitated!

Chapter Fourteen
The First Execution

I had brokered a deal with the government that if the PESA bill passed and I developed this system of equal justice, then the first use of the capital punishment system would be the execution of Carol's killer. The government was responsible for all ramifications concerning Robert Jones's sentence, which were to be updated and incorporated into the new PESA Act. And, this was to be done so that the execution could take place as soon as possible after the first Clobot was ready. The government had kept their end of the agreement. Robert Jones, over the many objections and appeals of his lawyers, was ready and waiting on death row for the first Clobot on May 19, 2053.

The first Clobot, nicknamed "RX," was completed on December 12, 2052, just over six months ago. However, with the ground breaking on January 8th of this year of the first CPC (Capital Punishment Center), the center was not completed and ready for use until April 24, 2053. The center then needs two weeks to design and produce the crime scene replica.

We are now ready for the new era of crime control to be put into practice.

Sunday, June 13, 2053 Steve and I returned to Los Angeles for our final check-up and testing the day before the execution. The stage crews were just putting on the finishing touches to the set. The original scene of the crime had been recreated. This was 14401 Hawktown Place, Houston, TX, June 14, 2043!

Mr. Robert (Empty {MT}) Jones has exhausted all forms of appeals: "cries of injustice, the unconstitutionality of this punishment system," and every other legal mumbo jumbo imaginable. All the games were over. Sunday, June 13, 2053, one day short of ten years since the night he brutally murdered Carol; Robert "Empty" Jones has only 32 hours to live! He will be executed ten years to the day and the exact hour he committed his crime.

Chapter Fifteen
CCID Working

Joshua Randelph and Betty Kindereth were married July 10, 2048. They had been high school sweethearts. Occasionally, they had dated others, but always came back to their first love.

Josh went into the military right out of High School in June of 2044. It was a heart breaking sendoff at the airport as Betty watched him walk away down the boarding ramp. Had it not been for the support of their many school friends and family, Betty would have been a basket case, and maybe still will be; four years is a long time.

That fall, Betty enrolled at University of Missouri Kansas City,

MO. Her goal was to become a "Paralegal." Who knows, someday, maybe even become a lawyer.

Josh and Betty wrote each other almost every day. Josh would go spend his leave time with Betty, except for some time with his family. Betty, too, would spend most of her vacation days and summers with Josh. These two were a match made in heaven.

These four years were the longest four years "ever." They both felt that time was standing still. They spent most of their time together discussing and planning the first thing they would get married when Josh got back home. They both agreed on a small wedding with only family and a few friends. They were all set if only time would cooperate.

Time does have a way of working out all our yearnings, desires, cravings….I'm being redundant, aren't I? It prepares us by teaching us to have hope, respect, and patients. And, four long years can really put these to the test.

Josh was discharged shortly before Betty's graduation. He returned home and got his own place: of course, he chose one with Betty in mind. One that she would love to live in and just about the same distance to both their parents houses in Kansas City suburbs.

Graduation came and Josh, along with both their families, was present and very proud.

Josh and Betty were married a month later, in that small ceremony they had agreed on. After a Honeymoon cruise to the Bahamas and a week they will never forget, it was time to return and dive into the real world.

Josh had spent his four years as a "grunt" in the military and did not get any special training that would help him get employment when he returned to civilian life. He had to take whatever was available and bounced from job to job.

Betty was able to get a job as a paralegal at a prestigious law firm, Shankel, Handly and Parsons Attorneys at Law. Her excellent income was a big help to compensate for the down time Josh had between jobs.

Their first child, beautiful Connie, was born Jan 6, 2050. Josh had considerable time off work as his job ended with the same old excuse, the company financial problems and they had to get rid of somebody. Josh always seemed to be that somebody. He never would admit or tell Betty it might have to do with his drinking.

Their second child was born August 17, 2051, Robert Lee Randelph. More time off led to more babysitting. Josh loved the kids but it was frustrating taking care of two young ones. However, his being able to watch the kids did save big bucks on childcare, which, when he did work barely covered that cost.

Josh drifted from one job to another. Between jobs Josh had a lot of time on his hands, even though he was busy watching the kids. But, this also, was time alone for him to think. Time that turned into guilt: he was the man of the house but playing housewife.

This situation began to eat at Josh. He was not the bread winner in the family: Betty was. He was not wearing the pants in in the family: Betty was. Betty was the one "bringing home the bacon." Josh was the one left to drown his problems in alcohol. Alcohol became his release: his comfort. His new buddy!

Josh became very quiet. He also developed a very short fuse with Betty and the kids. Josh turned even more to alcohol. He found alcohol to be a release for his guilt and resentment. But, it also became a catalyst for his anger. His anger had to have an outlet, which started manifesting itself in abuse.

Betty knew something was going on and tried to talk to Josh. But, every time she brought it up, it would turn from a discussion to a confrontation. It wasn't long before the confrontations became physical.

The abuse started with what he called "correction" for behavioral problems with the kids. It wasn't long before he turned on Betty as she tried to intervene on behalf of the kids. At first it was just pushing her away when she would intervene but it quickly escalated.

Josh's drinking was hidden from Betty at first but now became increasingly heavier and more frequent. Many times he would be drunk when she got home from work, and she began to notice bruises on the children. There is no excuse that a two and a three-and-a-half year old should have this many bruises.

Oh, yes, there was always the excuse of them falling, running into something, or from their hitting one another with their toys. That is when accusations entered the arguments. A mother will not stand for her kids to be abused!

First, there was the pushing. It wasn't long before the pushing escalated into a slap. Josh always came back pleading for forgiveness. Betty always forgave him, at first, for family's sake and because she loved Josh.

However, by the time of their fifth Wedding Anniversary, the slaps soon turned to a punch. Welcome to "living happily ever after!" Then, more punches. It wasn't long until Betty endured her first beating.

The beatings became more frequent, as well as, severe. The spanking or hitting of the kids also became more frequent and severe. Always, there was alcohol involved.

"911, may I help you?"

"Yes, please send help."

"What is your problem?"

"My husband just beat me and the kids," Betty said sobbing.

"Where is he now?" was the response from the dispatcher.

"I'm not sure. I locked the kids and me in our bedroom. I'm calling from there."

The dispatcher didn't hesitate and said, "Stay on the phone: I am sending help. Do not unlock the door! Help will be there soon." She went on to ask, "Do you need medical attention?"

"I'm not sure," Betty said.

It wasn't but a few minutes until Betty could hear sirens getting closer and closer. The next thing she heard was,

"Police Officer" shouting from outside the front door, "Police, open the door."

Betty opened the door to the bedroom and looked very carefully but did not see Josh anywhere. She then hurried to the front door to open it as the Police once again pounded on the door and demanded it be opened.

Two Police Officers immediately

assured Betty that she was safe and said,

"Where is your husband?"

"I don't know!"

At that time, Josh came in the back door and walked into the living room. He looked very puzzled at what was going on. Looking confused, he said,

"YOU CALLED THE COPS?" It was more a statement of disbelief than a question.

"I can't take it anymore, Josh." Betty cried, with tears streaming down her face.

Josh was immediately handcuffed and arrested. After a period of time he was sentenced to 2 years in jail. The

Judge agreed to a suspended sentence if Josh would complete mandatory counseling.

Josh agreed and underwent counseling.

****

Carlos Alvaresario headed out to meet his buddies for what is to be the biggest score of his life. Theirs was a very well planned burglary. No one at home and the jackpot was huge.

As he approached the designated meeting place Carlos had a feeling that he did not recognize. Somewhere deep inside there was a twinge that gave him a feeling of discomfort about the situation. Was there a flaw in their planning? Were they walking into a trap? What's going on? What's wrong?

The closer Carlos got to the meeting spot, the stronger the feeling inside. As he rounded the corner and saw his buddies the feeling became so strong that it almost make him sick, even though he knew the feeling was not in his stomach.

Carlos became very nervous at what was about to happen. He had a strong feeling that what was about to take place he didn't want to be part of. There was even a sense that this might not be the right thing to do. For the first time Carlos had a feeling of right and wrong.

Carlos was becoming very confused. He had never considered

whether his actions were the right or wrong thing to do: only, was it fun or was there money in it.

His buddies were all hyped up and ready to roll. They had visions of a humongous score.

Carlos greeted them, but not with the enthusiasm they were experiencing, or what they expected from him. Several noticed that something was different about Carlos.

The so-called leader, Jamie, detecting the same thing, asked, "Hey, bro, what's going on?"

Carlos, still unsure himself of what was happening, said, "I don't know. I just don't think I feel up to it tonight."

"What'a ya mean? Ya sick?"

"I guess so. I just can't do it." Carlos replied as he turned and started for home.

"Well, it's your loss bro. Maybe you don't have the guts for the big time." Jamie shouted as several others chimed in with their slams.

The farther Carlos got away from them the better he felt. He had a feeling deep within that he had done the right thing. For once, Carlos had the feeling that life was not all about fun and money. Carlos felt there was more to life and that he had done the "right thing!"

Carlos' life had a big turnaround that night. He started considering others more than himself. He became very close to his parents instead of playing them. Carlos loved his family, got a job, and did everything he could to help support and ensure his brothers and sisters did not go down the same path he had chosen. The CCID's moral input into Carlos' soul gave him a new life. Carlos became a very productive member of society.

Chapter Sixteen

Carol's Revenge

The predator takes on many forms. Some seem so innocent. But, still the need for survival is always there; no matter the form.

I walked onto the set and immediately a wave of terror took over my whole being. I could feel the same emotions welling up as if it were that very night ten years ago. I could hear Carol pleading not to hurt us, and then her cries for mercy as he brutally attacked and murdered her in cold blood. I can see him standing in the bedroom doorway with that look of "victory." Now thinking, that even his perceived victory looks like an intended world conqueror, such as, "Hitler" or "Attila the Hun," might have had after a victory in a great battle. I can still see Carol's blood running down his face and his tongue flicking out to catch the drops, in defiance of any humanity that might attempt to live in this animal. Now, ten years later, as I relive that night from beginning to end, my whole being is still crying out in pain, exploding into a plethora of emotions: love, adornment, happiness, fear, rage, pain, and finally hatred! I just sank to the floor and cried out at him, venting what I was unable to do that night. Then, as I have done so many times before, I just wept uncontrollably!

However, this is the day. Not only will the new era in crime control be ushered in, but justice and revenge for Carol and for me will also be served. I will be the one to throw the switch to put the "set" into motion. Now that "Empty's" execution is to be carried out, my revenge, an "eye for an eye," is being fulfilled. He may be "Empty." But, I am FULL!

Empty is led onto the stage blindfolded. Even in the face of execution he is arrogant and defiant. He has never even admitted to the crime: these were "trade secrets" he claimed. He never showed one ounce of remorse but, on the contrary, only spoke of how all those "bitches" deserved what they got. His body motion is undeniable of this fact: his face still twisted in his animalistic scowl. Even as his blindfold is being removed, he curses humanity and all it stands for.

"Go ahead, put me in the gas chamber, the electric chair, or hang me: see if I care. I will just laugh in your face as you strap me in!" He snarled.

The blindfold falls to the floor as the guards leave. Empty is alone to face the consequences of his actions. Empty, now able to looks around for the first time at his execution chamber, is not sure of what was happening. Not seeing the expected electric chair, gas chambers, or a hanging platform for the first time there is a hint of confusion and incredulity on his face.

That night, the headlights were very bright on the dark road in the backwoods. Rounding the bend, there he stood. Tall. Majestic. At least a twelve-pointer. Frozen! Eyes fixed on the lights! Unable to move. Waiting for the impact. The impact, that is sure to come.

Then looking around at the set, he shouts, "Hey, what the hell is going on here?" He continues, really confused, "What are you trying to pull? I recognize this place!" For the first time he unconsciously admits his guilt.

For the first time there was fear in his eyes as he screams out,

"GET ME OUTTA HERE!" With the situation beginning to set in he demands, "You can't do this to me, I have rights!"

"Empty" has just come face to face with reality: criminals, such as he, have no rights. All rights are relinquished upon conviction, and only "justice" remains. For the first time, in many face to-face encounters, Empty's scowl turns into a look of puzzlement. A sign of fear creeps in at the corner of his eyes. UNSURETY! UNCERTAINTY! INSECURITY! And, finally, DOUBT has replaced arrogance, control, domination and assurance. He falls to the floor as he realizes he is no longer in control and that fear has taken over.

Now, in this sub-human, this animal, in the end, just as will happen to all criminals, Empty is brought to his knees!

Empty realizes there is someone else in the room that is approaching him. He thinks that his demands to get him out of there have been met. Slowly he raises his head to look at the person that is now standing in front of him. His eyes rise slowly to meet the eyes of the one whom he thought was there to rescue him, but his gaze only becomes fixed on the glare of the one who once was his victim.

Empty is now experiencing an emotion he has never had to deal with before: horror! Now, the one standing before him is in control and has the "Empty" look in her eyes. A look that produces the horror that is in him.

Empty is looking into the eyes of Carol, who experienced his horror and is now inflicting it upon the animal that gave it to her.

With terror bursting from his face, "MT" is now trembling. He jumps to his feet and tries to defend himself, only to find that he is no match for his former victim. The strength that he once used to bully and overcome his victims is now useless. The power he wielded over Carol and me that night is no match against this Carol, this night. He is weak and defenseless against RX, the Robotic Executioner, the CloBot. He turns to run to another part of the house but is immediately stopped by Carol. Carol drags him toward the bedroom: the execution chamber!

What the….what's happening?

What are you doing? Who are you?" he screamed.

Now for the first time in his life he was forced to utter words that had never been in his vocabulary: "Help, help me!" Those were Robert Jones's last words!

I think there is a feeling that it was finally over. Robert Jones has been RX-ecuted! I think that now Carol can finally rest at peace. I no longer had to wonder what would happen if, by some slight chance, Empty would get another trial or stay of execution. I no longer had to worry that he might escape and once again reek horror on another victim. I did feel better. I felt some kind of relief, a kind of peace. I no longer had to fear!

It is finally over; nature has received its recompense.

Chapter Seventeen

Justice Applied

While we are in the process of producing a number of CloBots, to be shipped around the country to various law enforcement and government agencies, RX has a busy schedule ahead of it. There are more than 200 inmates waiting on death row to be executed for their crimes. It would still be a long, drawn-out process as each case is brought before the courts to see if the method of execution could legally be changed from the prescribed method, I.e., Gas Chamber, Electric Chair, or Hanging. The criminals' lawyers are doing their best to fight for the original execution method assigned by the courts. These liberals, left over from the old school of crime and punishment, fought hard against any change that would bring them into the new era of dealing with criminals: they were opposed and did not want anyone to die by "RX-ecution." Another obstacle we had to face was that the CloBots could only be used if skin, hair, blood, or other trace samples from the victim were still available. Otherwise, RX could not be programmed and the original style of execution remains. The good news is that anyone committing a capital punishment offense after the date of approval of PESA will fall under its guidelines and no court delays would apply.

So, for the next year, RX was doing only two or three executions a month, depending on the courts and the time required for set preparations. As with the first "RX-ecution," all following executions were televised through closed circuit television's paying audience. Televising executions was designed to have a significant impact on the criminal. Firstly, it is to let them know that they can no longer torture, mutilate, and kill people without that same criminal act becoming their very own punishment: revenge for the victim. "What goes around, comes around," as the old saying goes. Criminals should now start getting the message that they can no longer vent their hatred and total disregard for the law on an innocent society.

The second CloBot was ready just over a month after the original on January 24, 2053 and was sent to the East Coast execution facility that was just about completed. The third followed within another thirty days or less as the pace of production began picking up. Now, we have started supplying local law enforcement agencies with the CloBots. There were orders coming in from all over the world as law enforcement and government agencies can see the effectiveness the CloBots can bring to fighting crime.

As time passed, the effectiveness of the CloBots seemed to have the desired effect on crime. We now have CloBots that would be on a crime scene within a matter of hours, and in the future we hope within minutes. With a CloBot on the scene, in many cases, when a trace sample from the perpetrator was available, the perpetrator's likeness was reproduced within minutes and broadcasted across the nation via the news media. Many times the "perps" had a criminal history and not only was their face, but their name as well as their criminal history was immediately part of the broadcast. This instant national exposure resulted in many criminals being apprehended within hours, preventing them from inflicting further crimes or suffering upon the people.

******

Candice Callahamer's choice to have the implant was a life saver for her. Her party life led her deep into alcohol, then into drugs. Her need for drugs led her into stealing from work and even selling her body. She was on the road to total destruction.

Just as anyone else who had the implant device, Candy could no longer participate in her former life style. She had undergone a very complete drug rehabilitation program. She felt clean for the first time in a very long time. She also felt good inside about herself and the kind of life she was now living.

Candy was even given a second chance at her original place of employment. Work became a means for life not life itself. Candy was a happy member of society now.

Chapter Eighteen
Lingering Crime

Joshua and Betty have been married for just over six years now. Having spent the last few years of their marriage in a troubling relationship due to Josh's drinking, which resulted in physical abuse to Betty and the children, Betty had to have the police and courts intervene. Josh has now spent the last year in court appointed counseling and alcohol recovery programs and is now ready to move back home and restore their marriage.

The court gave Josh a probation period of six months for their marriage to work without any alcohol or abuse to Betty and the children. If Josh does not violate the courts probation, the court would not impose any further requirements and he would be released from any further appearances.

Things went well for a period of time; even completing the six months the court mandated. However, Josh, once again had employment problems. He honestly tried everything he could muster to be a good husband, provider and father. But, time after time of job rejection and being unable to be the provider for his family, it began to take its toll on the marriage.

Slowly, Josh started to have a beer to cool off and to calm down his frustrations. It wasn't long before it became necessary to have much more to placate him.

Again, Betty knew something was

going on and tried to talk to Josh. But, every time she brought it up, as in had in the beginning, it would turn from a discussion into a confrontation. The drinking had once again become very heavy.   Again, the confrontation became physical.   They quickly escalated to him being drunk when Betty got home from work and immediately and argument would ensue and the physical abuse returned as before: not only with Betty, but also with the children.

A mother will not stand for her kids to be abused!

Once again after a violent argument, Josh went into a drunken rage and gave a brutal beating to Betty and the kids. She had no choice but to call.

"911, may I help you?"

"Yes, please send help."

"What is your problem?"

"My husband just beat the kids and me."

"Where is he now?"

"I'm not sure. I locked me and the kids in our bedroom. I'm calling from there."

"Stay on the phone, I am sending help," the person on the other end of the line said. "Do not unlock the door! Help will be there soon. Do you need medical attention?"

"I'm not sure," Betty said.

Within minutes Betty could hear sirens getting closer and closer.

Then there was urgent pounding on the front door and a Police Officer shouting: "Police! Open the door!"

Betty opened the door and the officer assured her she was safe. He wanted to know where her husband was.

"I don't know," she said.

Josh, staggered in from the garage when he realized all the commotion was happening in his house. Looking thoroughly confused and having trouble processing what was going on and seeing the Police, he said:

"YOU CALLED THE COPS?"

Just as it had been before, it was more of statement of disbelief than a question.

"This can't keep happening. I can't take it anymore, Josh. You have to get help."

This being the second offence, the court was not playing any more games with Josh. The court sentenced Josh to no family contact until the completion of alcohol treatment and anger management counseling. After completion of treatments he was to serve three to five years in jail for the abuse to his family.

The court suspended the three to five years jail sentence for a one year supervised visit with Betty and the kids upon successful completion of the treatment programs.

Chapter Nineteen
Moving On With Life

We saw that within several years after the implement of PESA, with effective results from both the implant device and the terminal device, people were becoming more secure in their feeling and surroundings. Statistically, crime was on a downward trend in the inner cities. You could see the beginning of the movement on neighborhood streets at night. People were not afraid to go out of their houses after dark. Once again, mothers were beginning to allow their children to go to the corner market, the drug store, or the café. "Safe," and "secure" were once again words in the family vocabulary used in a positive way. And by New Year's 2057 people were out in the streets, unafraid, into the wee hours of the morning: celebrating.

And, as expected, happening even quicker than we thought, there were virtually no capital offenses occurring. There were even very few felonies occurring. We now had CloBots walking many of the beats that policemen once walked: policemen, who were now free of risking their lives every day to some drug crazed addict. Policemen, who now knew they would go home every evening after work to their loved ones. Yes, the CloBots are here and the criminals are just about gone!

******

I often wonder to myself if this is

really happening or if it is it just my imagination. Have we really, for the first time since the dawning of time, found a way to control "crime?" Are we really able to control or to entirely do away with this plague of crime that, until recently, reached the point of saturation in our communities? It just seemed too good to be true.

******

As crime started to become a thing of the past, I, once again, was able to get on with my life. I resumed my work for WOSE full-time instead of a part-time basis. I am still very much involved with the CloBot project. But, I feel I can once again move on to another project and be free to establish a relationship without the fear of it being destroyed in the blinking of an eye by some deranged individual.

I still found it hard to even consider another woman in my life instead of Carol. Over the next year, I did not do much dating, but did meet a young woman to whom I was attracted. Not unlike Carol, Sandra Hallinger is gorgeous. Sandy stands five foot five, slender, blond with deep, iridescent blue eyes. "Sans," as I call her, is a wonderful, beautiful woman. Sans, too, knew the heartache of losing her soulmate. She had been through too much tragedy in her life. Her husband, Jerry, had been killed by a crazy gunman in a bank holdup. Jerry was killed in cold blood for no reason other than he was just in the wrong place at the wrong time. He was there to open a new account and start saving for the future. His future was erased in a moment by the flash of a gun and the stinging of a bullet.

Sans also feels a sense of peace now that crime is becoming more and more invisible on the streets. The attraction grew between us into a solid love for one another. I, once again, was able to find a person whom I thought was the one I wanted to spend the rest of my life with and with whom I could have children. We were married Saturday, August 24, 2057, a year and three months after we met: at the ripe old age of thirty-four.

Having sold my house in The "Northsides," we purchased a home on the east side of Houston, out in the Deer Park area, to be closer to the water. This was a two story Tudor located at #16 Ocean View Place in the South Shore subdivision. We picked this one because it not only the best view but was also close to a community playground for the kids…..we're working on that!

Over the next five years, we had two children, first, a boy, Sean Russell, and then, a girl, Carol Maddisen. Maybe we weren't the Harrietts, but Sans and I loved the life we were finally able to rescue from the turmoil of a crime-infested world and to be firmly planted in the new world, which I have been blessed to be part of its creation.

Can life really return to normal and be this good? I really hope so!

Chapter Twenty
Crime's Last Hurrah

Crime statistics were very impressive. There had been a steady decline across the board in every type of crime documented. But, like everything else in life, the lack of crime is not a given. There were forces at work promoting crime, as well as the forces working for it prevention and ultimate eradication.

Joshua Randelph completed his intense abuse counseling which took about three months. After that, he was to meet once a week, along with Betty, for the next year.

It was mandatory for Josh not to have any abuse episodes during this period, or his original jail sentence would become effective. Josh did very well during this time. He did not, however, give up drinking entirely. But, he was able to control his drinking so as not to send him off the deep end. I do think it was more through fear of jail than through desire to do what was right.

It was now almost two years since Josh's arrest. Josh as able to find steady work, although it was not lucrative as for as income went, but, it seemed to give Josh a sense of worth. They were approaching their eighth Wedding Anniversary, just two days away. Josh was in a celebratory mood. Celebrations can be fun, but they sometimes get out of hand, too.

It was no problem for Josh to ease

back into drinking. So for the next two days, Josh drank almost non-stop. It wasn't long before the kids began to get on his nerves. It was easy to also return to his former methods of dealing with it.

Betty was quick to confront Josh this time and threaten him that she would not hesitate to call the police. Josh did not take threats very well. He lashed out at Betty and one blow followed another. This was probably the worst beating she had endured. However, the kids were old enough to run away.

That is exactly what they did. They ran to the neighbors and told them what their "daddy" was doing. The neighbor phoned the police!

The police arrived without sirens while Josh was still ranting and raving. Betty lay helpless on the floor. She was bleeding from her eyes, nose, and mouth. Every part of her body ached from the blows she received.

The police could hear the loud commotion inside and knew what was going on. They were required to announce before entry but there was no law about how close the two could be together.

"Police, open up!" Was the announcement as the door flew open! Two officers stormed into the room and tackled Josh. They were the same two officers that made his first arrest. This time they had no mercy. Josh was thrown to the floor so hard that he thought every bone in his body was broken. Both officers were on top of him, forcing his arms behind him and cuffing him.

Even being drunk to the point it was hard to stand, Josh knew this was the end of the line.

The judge had no mercy and told Josh she would love to send him to prison for life but that, according to the law, she could not. Then the judge said,

"In lieu of a life in prison, we now have available a system that will rehabilitate you. I sentence you to receive the CCID implant. This implant you will have in you for life! It will give you a life rather than sending you where there is no hope for life."

Josh was immediately implanted with the device. He was not allowed to return home until the device was able to make major changes in his behavior. Josh spent the next year in a halfway house.

Josh was not able, through an internal moral feeling, to return to drinking: he came to realize it was wrong for him. He also dealt with his anger and feelings of inadequacies.

Betty and the kids visited Josh every weekend. Children need their fathers. Betty, even after all she endured, still loved Josh. They all knew it was just a matter of time that they would be able to "live happily ever after."

On July 10, 2058, Josh, Betty, and the kids celebrated their 10th Wedding Anniversary happily!

Chapter Twenty-one

Déjà vu

THEN IT HAPPENED! Out of nowhere, a woman in Los Angeles was brutally raped and murdered with her husband tied up in the other room. The whole city was in a state of shock. It had been over five years since the last murder and the residents were at rest. However, it didn't take any time at all for fear and unrest to sweep throughout the city. The residents were in a panic. Everyone was afraid that their original fears about the CloBots were coming true. That the CloBots were just a fad, and that after a period of time, criminals would find a way of getting around them. So, we not only had the problem of a murder, the first in over five years, we also had the lack of confidence of the people to deal with. Since the last murder in July of 2054, people hardly even said the word "murder." In light of this newest crime, just how to convince the people that everything will be alright only added to the problems of figuring out how and why this happened. The people must be reassured that the CloBots can do their job, preventing crime and maintaining peace. That the person would be caught as in the past by the CloBots and punished!

The Los Angeles National Punishment and Enforcement Department (NPED) office, which was now integrated into the Los Angeles Police Force, called and requested my assistance. I immediately flew to Los Angeles to aid in any way I could to help solve the murder as well as determine what went wrong with the system. When I got there I went directly to the Chief of Police, Bob Stalley, who said,

"We have sealed off the crime scene, and the body has not been removed." He further stated that a CloBot had been brought in but there wasn't any suspect yet. I said to him,

"I need to go to the crime scene."

When we arrived at the crime scene there were people everywhere. Reporters were pushing and shoving, shouting questions from all around us, trying to get something for a "breaking story" news flash. The main question, shouted over and over by everyone, was the one Bob was asked by a reporter standing in our way.

"Should the people once again lock themselves in and arm themselves?" and "Are the CloBots no longer effective?" This sawed-off, shrimp of a reporter asked in an accusing way.

It was hard to push our way past this guy, and the many other reporters, and the crowd that gathered to see what was happening. We entered through the front door into the living room. The home was in a very nice neighborhood. Security was not high in any area anymore but this neighborhood did have all the items that were being used today. It was a gated community. They did have a guard at the gate. The home itself did have an alarm system. However, like so many around the country now, many people did not rely on these systems anymore. So, I thought to myself, "Why did this happen and how did it happen?"

"The husband is in the hospital," Bob said, "I think he will live."

Bob then pointed to his right, to a hallway and said "The wife is in the bedroom, on the bed." He hesitated, like he did not want to go in there again.

When I walked into the bedroom I immediately fell to my knees. I became dizzy and momentarily passed out. When I came to there were a couple of Policemen who had picked me up and put me in a chair over in one corner, standing next to me with their hands on my shoulder to be sure I could sit. I was trembling all over. I slowly got up and walked toward the bed again. There she lay, covered with blood. She had been stabbed many, many times all over her upper torso. The look of horror still permanently etched on her face. Her eyes still open with a look of unbelief at what was happening. As I turned I looked her in the eyes, which once again, hurled me back sixteen years to that horrible night June 14, 2043. I could see Carol lying there on the bed, just as I had seen in the police photos during the trial of Empty Jones. How could this have happened again? Could there ever be another person so devoid of humanity, such as Empty? Again, my heart felt as if it were being torn from my chest as it was that unthinkable night, again, flashing before my eyes.

We combed the house from front to back and top to bottom with a fine tooth comb, looking for that little something that would lead us to the person or persons who did this. Prints were taken from everything. Hairs, skin, fibers were taken from every room. CloBots tried reproducing the perpetrator from every piece of evidence, but the only persons in the house that night, according to the evidence, were the victims.

There has to be more! We've got to be over-looking the obvious. We spent another three days going over the house with a magnifying glass. No one was getting any sleep. Everyone was exhausted. Nerves were on edge. The slightest thing would set someone off on a tirade. Still nothing!

I agreed to stay for another two weeks to aid in any way I could, but I had to return to Houston after that. I called "Sans" every chance I got, not only to get myself out of the horror of the memories that kept flooding back, but to get relief for a few minutes of this intense, exhausting investigation.

Over the next two weeks we fed every thread of evidence into the CloBots. Again, we were up against a brick wall as everything produced a replica of the two victims. It appears that nothing or no one was in that house the night of the murders except the victims, which is impossible. Or, was it murder-suicide? I called Bob over and said,

"Bob, do you think this could possibly be a murder-suicide?"

"No way!" he replied without hesitation, then went on to explain, "That is always one of the first things we look at in a crime like this. We looked at this from every angle to see if that was possible.”

I asked, “Why not.” wanting an explanation.

“There is no way for anyone to inflict upon themselves the number and type of wounds the husband sustained while in a conscious state,” Bob, said. Then, he continued by adding, “Yet, the husband cannot provide us with any information concerning the person that did this. He can only remember he and his wife preparing to Bar-b-que on the patio and his wife having gone into the house.” After checking his iNote, an electronic note pad all policemen now carry, he went on to say, “The last thing the husband remembers is, as he was leaning over to light the coals, his wife telling him the meat was ready to cook and then feeling a sharp pain in the back of his head." Bob said the weapon that had been used was found next to him.

Bob went on to say, "There was a trail of blood from the patio into the living room where the perp must have dragged the husband at some point. Because it looks like the real beating occurred in the living room." Explaining how they feel the events happened, Bob said,

"While the wife was in the kitchen, the perp approached the husband from the rear and struck him in the back of the head with a large rock from the flower bed. The perp then went into the house, the wife thinking the footsteps were that of her husband coming to get the meat, he grabbed her from behind and forced her to get some panty hose and tie her husband's hands and feet. There were a second set of bindings, so we assume the perp himself made sure the husband was securely tied up." Bob went on to say, "We believe he then took the wife to the bedroom to rape and murder her."

After this lengthy description, Bob also said that the rock was not the weapon to inflict all the wounds on the husband. But, the beating that took place inside, in the living room, was done with a poker from the fireplace.

Bob concluded by saying, "If his wife was the only other person there who beat her husband? Then who raped and murdered her? And if her husband raped and murdered her, how in the hell did he inflict that kind of damage on himself and still be able to tie himself up?" There had to be another person in that house who committed this crime!

After listening to Bob's gruesome account of the crime, I knew he was on tract but he really didn't understand the full scope of what went on. This crime was not that simple. This "perp" did not just come in and knock the husband out and then rape and murder his wife. This perp was an animal! This perp had no feelings for his victims. This perp was devoid of emotion. This perp was EMPTY!

Chapter Twenty-two
It's Not Over

I was scheduled to leave the next day. Friday, July 10, 2059, would be the last day that I could help here where the crime took place. I was packing and had the television on. There was one of those "talk shows" on but I really wasn't paying much attention because it was the same old subject "Better Sex with Your Wife." Then the interruption: "A special news report!" There has been another murder in Los Angeles. I gasped and reached to turn the TV up louder. The Special News Anchor said,

"Breaking story at this very moment, there is a report that another couple has been attacked, the wife is dead and the husband severely beaten. Stay tuned; as soon as more information becomes available, we will keep you updated."

I immediately called home and when Sans answered, I said,

"Have you heard the latest?"

"No, what?" was her reply. I went on to say,

"There has been another murder." I heard her gasp in horror. I said to her,

"Sans, be sure that you arm the alarm system and there is no way I can make the plane tomorrow. This is going to take some time to figure this one out." She responded, with disappointment in her voice and said,

"I know, you have to stay and do what you have to do." I responded by saying,

"Why don't you grab the next flight out and spend some time here?" I suggested.

"Not now, it would just be too much with the kids and I don't think Mom is up to handling them this soon after her surgery. Maybe if something doesn't break soon we'll come later." Softly, she whispered and said, "I love you, I wish I could be there!"

I arrived at the latest crime scene and it looked almost identical to the first one. Body position and method of attack on both the wife and husband were the same. The murder weapon used on the wife and the weapon used on the husband were also the same as previously used. There was no evidence of forced entry. Now, for the second time, there was no evidence of anyone other than the victims being in the house that night. Once again we had no suspects.

The press was clambering for information. The public was demanding an arrest. We had nothing! There was no information for the press and there was no suspect to arrest to satisfy the public. The city was at the point of hysteria. They knew we had a serial killer on our hands.

Weeks passed as we went through the same process of gathering evidence that we had done after the first murder. Only this time, we looked closer and included the whole block surrounding the scene of the crime. Still, everyone was at a dead end. Where is the key?

There has to be something we're missing. I took the pages of evidence from the first crime and put it alongside the mounting pages from the current crime scene. My eyes were getting blood shot from going over and over the same information. I felt I was getting light headed, and then it hit me! There was only one way this could have happened. So I called the Captain and said,

"I've got to move into the house, for a couple days, where the first murder occurred." I went on the tell him, "I also need you get me two CloBots, one from the original production and one from the latest production." He agreed, even though I would not tell him what I was up to.

Chapter Twenty-three
Testing the CloBot

I moved in and immediately went to work.

First thing was to check the ColBots and be doubly sure I had both an old version and the new version. This task was done rather quickly as I logged into the CloBotic Production Unit (CPU) at WOSE. I had also lobbied hard to have WOSE produce the CloBot units so that I could carefully monitor their production. Each CloBot is to have a production number issued and embossed on its buttock. The productions numbers would be assigned in the following manner:

1. Either the letter "A" for CloBot or "B" for Implant Device.
2. Last two digits for year of production.
3. Two digits for day of production.
4. Two digits for month of production.
5. Either the letter "O" for original unit or "U" for an updated unit.
6. Three digit number for production run.

I had easy access to all product information, including all CloBot production numbers. I downloaded the list of old and new production numbers. I compared the two units I had, and the numbers confirmed I had a first and a second version of the CloBots.

All the older or original RX versions, have to be manually deprogrammed after each use to restore them to their original state. The newer model, the RX2, has a built in deprogramming circuitry. If the older models were not deprogrammed properly, I think there could be a glitch in the cloning mechanism. That is the task at hand.

The original RX that was built to mimic Carol was also used in the first execution. After being used in a number of other executions, that unit is probably no longer in L.A. However, that may be the next thing that I will have to check out. Every unit's production number is supposed to be kept in a log, recording its whereabouts and activities at all time.

My first test was to see if the older units have a problem with the input port. These ports have a seal around them and I need to check the sustainability of these seals. I need to compare them to the new units which have a newer impregnable lifetime seal.

Performing different type stress tests on the seals revealed that the original units may be susceptible to penetration. This is not a definite determination of what happened, but it is a strong possibility.

Further testing eliminated the newer version CloBot the RX2 completely. I then turned my full attention to the older version RX. I activated with trace and deprogrammed time and time again, to no successful conclusion. Although, there were times it seemed there could be a contamination. Contamination would mean the sequence programming was not completely eradicated to the point that only the unit's basic program remained. This could be a major potential problem if this were to happen.

This is the only scenario that I have found that could answer what was happening. Also, if a CloBot was responsible for these crimes, it would have the potential to cover its tracks by assuming the identity of one of the victims, and therefore, it would only leave the prints of a victim. While its basic unit was damaged by the DNA of a perp that had been the victim of capital punishment, it still could function reasonably. However, it remains a killing machine!

This makes sense. A CloBot is responsible for these crimes. But, which CloBot and how did it get compromised? And, by whom was it compromised? I must find the answers to these questions. These answers will provide us with the identity of the perpetrator. However, I have my suspicions of whom, as to the how I have not figured out, yet. Is "Empty" getting his revenge?

The first thing I did the next morning was to call and inform Bob Stalley of my findings and my suspicions. Not understanding the minutiae of how it would be possible, Bob said,

"You really think that someone who was put to death over seven years ago can now be committing these crimes?"

"All I can say is that these are exact duplicates of the horrible crime I suffered and the way Carol was treated. Humanly, no, it isn't possible." I went on to further explain, "However, you add the element of the CloBot and what it is capable of doing, YES, I think that it is very possible. Perhaps, even probable!"

"Bob, can you check the reports from both crime scenes and see which of the victims had the greater number of prints at the scene?" I asked. Then, said,

"I need to locate the first RX that performed the execution of Robert Jones. I will get back to you shortly"

I hung up the phone and immediately logged into the National CloBotic Activity Control Center (NCACC) to check the whereabouts of

RX (Carol), the first production. To my surprise, this unit had been returned to Los Angeles about six months ago and should be in the central warehouse at NPED in Los Angeles. I am on my way!

After showing proper ID, a guard escorted me into the warehouse to find product number A141212OU001. The units are stored in sequence according to production number. There is an area for the CloBots and a large cabinet with multiple drawers for the Implant Devices. We went to the CloBots' area. All areas are sanitized, and cap, gown, and mask must be worn. The task of finding RX would be easy in storage because it would be the first one in line. I checked the number of the first CloBot; all CloBots were stored with their buttock facing out, and it was productions #A152401OU002.

I immediately gave the number to the guard, and we both started checking to see if RX had been stored out of sequence. The more we checked, the more frantic I became.

It wasn't long before I realized that my worst suspicions had come true. RX was not here and was out there; perhaps ready to commit another brutal killing. He must be found!

Chapter Twenty-four
Hunter or Hunted

I immediately called Bob and said,

"He is not here!"

"Who is not here?"

"Empty!" I shouted, then explained,

"I went to the warehouse to check and be sure the CloBot that was used in Robert Jones' execution was where it was supposed to be and it wasn't. We searched every CloBot in storage and according to the manifest RX was supposed to be here. It wasn't!"

"Well, do you think it could be out on assignment and it is just paperwork?

"No Bob there are built in safeguards against that type error. RX must have picked up some type trace evidence off a worker, cloned himself, and simply walked out unchallenged."

"What's our next step? How do we ever catch one of these, Hank?"

"That's what I have to figure out. I think this has now become a game to him. He knows I am the one who wreaked revenge on him so now he is trying to do the same to me."

"You mean, he is playing a cat and mouse game with you?"

"Yes, right now he can do whatever he wants whenever he wants."

"Well, who do we look for? Do

we have any idea what he looks like if he is walking the streets?

"At this time, Bob, I have no idea." Major mistake: we did not include a tracking device in the first ten units built as we did in all units after that. Is it possible that any one of these original units can be compromised like RX? Is it necessary to recall and destroy the first ten units? Or maybe even all the original units produced? I have some real heavy thinking to do. It's time I also contact Steve!

I hung up from Bob and dialed Steve's number,

"Hey, Hank, you making any headway out there in L.A?" Steve asked as he had checked the caller ID before answering.

"Not much. You heard about the second murder, didn't you?"

"Yea, you think they're tied together?"

"They're definitely the same killer. What's more I think it's a CloBot!"

"You've got to be kidding? There are protections in place." Steve said trying to reassure me.

"Not for the first ten units! But, I think it is RX number one," I said.

"How? Why do you say that?" Steve asked, very puzzled at what I said.

"I did some testing on both the old and new units and found that it is possible the old units could be compromised." I explained.

I then went on to tell Steve the whole situation and how the crime scenes were exactly as what Carol and I had experienced. I told him I was flying to Houston and would call him when I got in.

I flew back to Houston Friday May 24th to meet with Steve and get his thoughts on what could have gone wrong and also how to catch someone who is invisible? A CloBot is able, at any time, to change his appearance to any one of millions of people. He is invisible in plain sight!

The first thing I did was rent a car and head straight home. I had to see Sans. It had been almost six weeks since I had last seen her and the kids.

I spent that evening enjoying family bonding time: meal (at the dining room table), time just talking and sharing what is going on in each other's life, and a lot of hugging and kissing. I, also spent the next two days with them, going to the Zoo, fun time in the park, and out to eat, several times.

First thing Monday morning, I called Steve and told him I was on my way to the office to meet with him. He said he had a light schedule and I could have all the time I needed.

Driving the streets of Houston isn't any better than L.A. during rush hour. It seemed like everyone was headed to the same place I was going. Bumper to bumper. Stop and go. I didn't have the radio on because I wanted to get back into the mode of trying to figure out what happened and how to approach Steve.

A drive that normally took forty-five minutes wound up taking an hour and ten minutes. My nerves were quite rattled. I couldn't even find a parking place that was less than a three-minute walk. Great start for a Monday!

I passed through all security check points and headed straight for Steve's office. I walked in expecting a big smile and a warm hug, but to my surprise got neither. Steve was pacing, and when I knocked on the door jamb he turned with this expression of deep anguish on his face. I said,

"What in the world is wrong? Aren't you glad to see me?

"Did you hear?" He gasped.

"Hear what?"

"There's been another murder!"

"I figured it was only a matter of time," I said, "that is why I came back to Houston, to see if the two of us can figure this thing out."

"You still don't understand." Steve blurted out!

"Understand what?" I said, getting a little up tight.

"Here! Here in Houston! The murder was here Friday night, but they just discovered it early this morning." Steve explained.

"What, how is that possible?" I, said, in total shock!

"I don't know, but it happened." Steve said, assuredly.

"Oh, God, RX must have followed me to Houston!" I cried out,

"He must have been on the same plane I was on." I said, trembling.

I still detected something in Steve's voice that he had more to tell me but was having trouble saying it. Steve, trying to be delicate said,

"There's more."

"What more?"

"It was the same setup a..a…as…Carol."

"Ya, I kind'a figured that. The two in L.A. had a great similarity."

"Well, this one was not only similar from what the news reports are saying." Steve went on to try and explain everything being reported. He, then said "But Hank" hesitating, trying to put the pegs in the right holes, then looking for the right words to explain, he was hesitant to continue…

"How are the news people tying this to Carol so quickly?" I interrupted, as he was still pacing the floor.

"Because,…because, Hank, it was at 14001 Cedar Ridge." Steve uttered, ever so softly.

Everything just went black!

The next thing I knew I saw Steve and his secretary kneeling and staring down at me. Both were saying, over and over, "Hank, Hank! Are you alright?"

The spinning began to decrease slowly, and the room and their faces started to come into focus. My head felt like it had been hit with an axe" splitting pain from front to back. They carefully eased me into a sitting position which helped with the spinning. The headache, not so much. After what seemed like hours, I was able, with their help, to get into a chair. They gave me all the time I needed to recuperate.

"Oh, my God, Steve, this animal is back. And he is wreaking revenge on anyone and everyone."

"I'm not so sure it's 'anyone' or 'everyone.'" Steve said hesitantly, and then went on to say,

"What if Empty thought you still lived at that address? Maybe he didn't know you moved and thought he was going to get you and your new wife?"

"So, the other two murders in L.A. were just warnings, and now he is going for the real thing?" I said, not knowing if it was a question or a statement.

"That is exactly what I think is happening!" Steve confirmed.

I immediately grabbed my phone and called Sandra. The phone rang and rang for what seemed forever: like she would never pick up.

"Hello, Hank. What's going on?" Sans asked.

"Sans, I want you to pack some bags for at least three or four days' stay. Please don't ask any questions! I will be there in about forty-five minutes to pick you and the kids up. Keep the kids in the house till I get there." I tried to be as calm as possible while still trying to give some sense of urgency.

"What is going on Hank? Where are we going?" Being totally confused, Sans, asked.

"I don't have time to explain right now. Please, just do as I say and I will explain everything when I get there. Lock the doors and set the alarm until I do get there. See you in forty-five."

I hung up so Sans would not try to question me further and also so she could get busy getting her and the kids ready. I told Steve I would call him so we can get together and figure this thing out. I turned and quickly left his office and the building.

Exactly forty-four minutes later I pulled into the driveway. I rushed into the house to find Sans and the kids ready and waiting in the living room. I immediately grabbed the bags and said, "Let's go!" as I turned for the front door.

Sans took Sean and Carol's hands and followed me out the door, not even looking back. We got in the car without a word being spoken. We left the house, and I drove in a zig-zag pattern getting out of our neighborhood and for another mile or two checking to be sure we were not followed. We left Houston and headed east.

"Where are we going?" Sans finally asked.

"New Orleans." I replied.

"What is going on Hank?" Sans asked, with caution in her voice, to protect Sean and Carol.

"What happened in L.A. has happened here."

"What's that got to do with us?" Sans asked with this puzzled look on her face.

"Not only here in Houston, but at my old address, my old house! It was an attempt to either get me or send me a direct message that we're next." I spelled out as plain as I could for Sans.

"It is the original perp who has taken over the original CloBot, RX. Somehow it became compromised with Robert Jones' blood and has now permeated the brain so it thinks it is Robert Jones." I explained further.

"Does that mean we all are in dang…….?" Sans couldn't finish the word but I knew what she meant by the fear in her eyes.

"That is why we are taking this little vacation with the KIDS." I said, with emphasis on KIDS so they would hear and think this was a fun trip. It seemed to be working by the laughter in the back seat.

"I will call Steve as soon as we get settled in and we will get together to figure this thing out. You…, we all will be safe in New Orleans!" I said, trying to comfort Sans as much as I could.

We settled into a nice, quite little Bed & Breakfast on Bourbon Street. Here, we would blend in and be as invisible as Empty seemed to be.

Chapter Twenty-five
The Hunter

First thing after checking in, I called Steve and told him we were safe. We were just under three hundred fifty miles from Houston, and Steve agree that if we both drove about three hours, we could meet somewhere in between. We agreed that Jennings, LA was about half way for each of us. We agreed to meet at Ten A.M. Wednesday, giving me a day to reassure Sans and to let the kids know this is going to be a fun time. I told Steve I would call him and let him know where to meet in town.

I was up early on Wednesday morning and went downstairs to get a cup of coffee that the hostess kept brewed almost twenty-four hours a day. Like many folks, I do my best thinking over a cup of strong, black coffee. After leaving Sans a note about where I would be, I took a pad and pencil downstairs with me. After a couple hours I had jotted down a number of thoughts I wanted to discuss with Steve.

Sans came down about seven-thirty, looking like she had been up for hours, ready to hit the road. What a beauty. Adorable!

"Got any of that good stuff left?" She asked.

"I think I just left enough for one more cup." I assured her.

"The kids are still asleep so I thought I would run down and grab a quick cup and make sure you were still here.”

“I thought I would head out about eight. That would give me plenty of time to find a good place to spend the day with Steve and figure out our next move,” I told Sans as I stood and put my arms around her. She just snuggled close as she could, being careful not to drench me with her cup of gold. Also, not to look like a couple of moonstruck teenagers in front of the other three house guest at the oversized dining room table.

After telling her I would be upstairs shortly to kiss the kids, and her of course, since I didn't want to do it in front of the guest and really confirm to them we had gone off the deep end by acting like a couple of love-sick teens, especially at our ages. Sans knew she was number one on the kiss list. I then informed her,

"I packed a few things just in case this thing gets prolonged and we don't come up with any answers and have to work late into the night. I will call you."

"I hope not. That is that you don't have to spend the night. That might be hard to explain to the kids that daddy is off somewhere else when he is supposed to be here having fun." She stated as she turned to head back upstairs.

I finished my third cup of coffee and made a few more notes before heading upstairs. When I got to our room Sean and Carol were watching cartoons as Sans sat nearby reading a book. I went over and tickled both until they were pleading for mercy. I gave them both a big hug several kisses goodbye, and told them how much I loved them. Sans was next, not for tickling, but to tell her how much I love her and to kiss her goodbye, well, maybe a couple kisses or so.

After pulling myself away from my three favorite people in the world, I headed downstairs and out to the car. I headed west on Interstate 10 to Jennings, LA, at 8:05 A.M. I kept going over the notes I had made this morning, hoping to get a better picture of the task ahead. My mind was so busy it seemed that I had just started when I saw a sigh that said "Jennings 12 miles."

Jennings is a lovely old town that

was settled in the late eighteen hundreds with a population over ten thousand. I drove slowly around town, trying to choose a place that we could spend all day for a solution to our problems. After scouting out many restaurants, shopping centers, and hotels, I decided the library would be the best place. I phoned Steve, whom I had warned to start out in a zig-zag pattern, like we had done, to be sure he wasn't tailed and gave him the address of the library. Steve was still about thirty minutes out. I grabbed another cup of coffee at a convenience store, parked outside the library and waited for Steve.

Steve drove up and fortunately found a parking spot two cars down from where I was parked. He got out and came and tapped on the passenger's side window. I got out and we shook hands and went inside the library.

Steve opened his briefcase and pulled out a very large folder of papers along with his laptop. His laptop contained all the files downloaded from the main computers at WOSE concerning the development of the CloBot. He had a schematic of the internal electronic workings: the brains of the unit. There were detailed drawings of the proposed construction: showing the mechanics of the unit. And, there were photos, from day one until completion on the assembly line, of the CloBot. This was going to be an all-nighter. We packed up the stuff and headed for the door to find a room for the night. I pulled my phone out of my belt case and called Sans.

"I was expecting you'd call." Sans said with disappointment in her voice, not that I called but she knew what I was going to say.

"I'm sorry, honey, but there is just too much to even think we can get it done tonight. I hope to be there by late afternoon. Kiss the kids. I love you." I hung up, and we walked toward downtown to find the nearest hotel.

Both Steve and I, grabbed a cup of coffee from the coffee bar inside the hotel lobby and headed straight to my room. We wasted no time getting set up and going through the mound of paperwork and computer information. I took the paperwork and Steve dove into the computer stuff. We both were looking for what we believed there had to be: a weakness in the CloBot!

We were so engrossed in what we were doing we hardly spoke a word, and before we knew it we worked long past lunch. We probably would have gone even longer if nature hadn't called because of all the coffee. We decided a break would be the best thing and that it would also give us a chance to discuss what we may have found.

We found this little café that specialized in home cooking and the smell coming from it confirmed this was the place. I could swear that even my gut jumped with joy as we entered, and the bell on the door sounded "dinner time."

I had the 'Special of the Day,' beans and cornbread. Steve chose something more local….crawfish!

While we waited we discussed what we have looked at so far and if we felt there was anything of significance in it. I poured over the mechanical drawings of the unit paying special attention to the seals around the electronic. There are four seals to protect the electronic workings of the unit.

The first seal is where the removable skull detaches from the head. The head contains the main electronic programming unit which is divided into two major sections: the Basic Behavioral Unit (BBU) and the Capital Punishment Unit (CPU), which has a small DNA input port with a fourth seal. The Compromise in this fourth seal is insignificant. This main unit is known as the brains of the CloBot. This first seal is the most important. If this seal is compromised, DNA could penetrate either or both parts of the main unit and alter its basic programming. Penetration here could cause the whole unit to be compromised. A compromise could occur when capital punishment is being inflicted upon the perpetrator.

The BBU is the mechanical functioning of the CloBot: walking, talking, seeing, etc. and only becomes active when the CPU is sensitized.

The CPU is the main unit of intent: the moral coding or intent of actions. The CPU is where the individual capital punishment specifics are programmed into the CloBot, activating the basic programming to perform the assigned task. The CPU interacts with the BBU to carry out physically what is required of the CloBot to perform assigned functions.

We also knew that desensitizing the CPU after it has completed its task does not affect the BBU (Basic Behavioral Unit) which returns to an inactive state. The DNA of the perp is entered into the Capital Punishment Unit. The perp's DNA activates the criminal actions that the perp inflicted on the original victim. These actions now become his own method of capital punishment. Once the task is finished, the CPU is desensitized.

The morphing programming unit is located in the lower part of the back of the head, which also has a DNA input port. The second and third seals are located in this area. The second seal is located around the DNA input port that activates the morphing programming unit. The third seal is between the morphing unit and the main programming unit. A compromise in either of these seals would be insignificant to actions.

Over a period of time, the penetration and convergence of an altered DNA would change the basic intent of the CloBot to that of the comprised DNA. This could be devastating. Steve and I agreed that the first seal must be the area of our full concentration.

After dinner we headed back to my room for some intense scrutiny of these seals. We spent the rest of the night looking at the first seal in particular, how it might be compromised, and, if so, how the DNA would penetrate it and become dominant over the basic programming. Hours passed and it seemed we were getting nowhere. We did agree that it was possible to penetrate the seal, but how someone's DNA could metastasize to envelop and penetrate the basic program and replace it with human programming was beyond our comprehension. Long after midnight we decided it would be better to start fresh the next morning because both our minds had shifted into neutral.

The next morning, we met, for breakfast, at the same café, where we ate dinner yesterday. Since dinner had been so good, we knew breakfast would be excellent. It was. We lingered over plenty of good, strong coffee, and the caffeine helped invigorate our thoughts with some fresh new ideas. Rest had been the best solution last night, for we both seems to be unable to pinpoint what might happen upon contamination. This is the first step in developing a solution.

After breakfast and a quick call to Sans to see how things were going, we headed back to the room.

We agreed that my earlier test had confirmed the problem with the seals and the possibility that if penetrated the DNA could compromise the unit. We both agreed that Empty's blood from when he was executed by RX had penetrated the first seal which then penetrated the main programming unit: one or both parts. The blood reached an area that is supposed to be sealed off and became part of the programming brain making a permanent link between the CPU and the brain. The sequencing programming had been contaminated to the point that the unit's basic programming was compromised. That is when the unit went rouge and left the warehouse. This was evident by the actions in the three recent crime scenes.

It was now putting into action the thoughts and intents of the compromised DNA. This was now becoming the brain and actions of Robert Jones. That is when it acted completely like a human being (only in a robot body). That is when Empty once again was walking the streets! RX was now a living, walking, talking killing machine: Robert 'Empty' Jones!

Chapter Twenty-six
The Hunt

How do you catch a CloBot? How do you catch a Clobot who has the ability to change its identity at any given moment or circumstance? How do you find someone that is invisible in plain sight? How do you know who is real and who is not?

If we can answer these questions, we will be able to catch and stop Empty from committing any further crimes.

Steve and I spent the rest of the morning and most of the afternoon trying to come up with a plan that would be able to find and stop or destroy the rogue RX CloBot.

How do you find someone that is invisible? In fact, I had no proof that it wasn't Empty sitting across from me in the likeness of Steve discussing how to catch himself. Well, other than the fact that we took every precaution to be sure Empty did not locate us and therefore, would be unable to replace either one of us.

Catching a Clobot is next to impossible….no, wait: it is impossible! We cannot waste our time searching the planet for someone whom we cannot put a particular face on at any given moment. In fact there is no way to even determine a CloBot from a human walking the streets. There must be another way. We must try other means.

Then a thought struck me, "To catch a CloBot you must be a CloBot!" Not a CloBot running the streets around the country looking for Empty, but a CloBot used as BAIT!

I told Steve what I was thinking and he said,

"That's it! Why did it take so long to realize that?"

"I don't know, sometimes you can't see the forest for the trees," I said. Then went on thinking out loud,

"We can't locate him but we can get him to locate us….or the one of us he is after."

"Yes, but you are no match for a CloBot, Hank."

"I know. That is why we will be CloBots. They will morph into Sans and me to draw out Empty. He will know by now he had the wrong address when he went to where he committed his first crime and will be intent on finding our new address and to come looking for us."

"That's great. However we will have to develop a defense program to go along with the offensive capital punishment program. This will be necessary to protect the CloBot from being destroyed by Empty's offensive skills." Steve explained.

"I agree. This program must give the CloBot the ability to defend itself and also to defeat and destroy the enemy. I don't think that would be that difficulty a task to write and program a couple CloBots with these skills. Time is of the essence!"

Our task here is finished. This sounds like a good plan. We packed our stuff, and before leaving, Steve called the Chief of Police in Houston to inform him of the plan and ask him to meet us at WOSE at 9 A.M. the next morning. While Steve called Houston, I called Bob Smalley in L.A. because of the two murders he was covering and told him the same things. He agreed to fly out tonight and be at WOSE in the morning. We will walk them through the plan at that time. We were all set. We both grabbed our things and headed out the door: Steve to Houston and me to New Orleans. Things were looking brighter, even though the sun had set and darkness had pushed the daylight into hiding.

Chapter Twenty-seven
Setting the Trap

Empty sat staring intently at the security gates just a few hundred yards down Shore Cliff Drive. He had just finished his third phone call, in as many days, to #16 Ocean View Place: no answer. So, he just sat and patiently waited until someone was home at their affluent South Shore subdivision home. He had been here for days but time means nothing to a CloBot. He knew Hank would eventually return home.

Having returned to Houston, but not to our home, we stayed with Steve and Maddisen, whom Steve married six months after Carol's death. We felt safe here for Empty would be searching and expecting us at our new place. Sans and Maddi had, also, become the best of friends, and the kids thought she was their aunt. Steve and I were free to go to work as long as we were careful to not be too visible.

Since the girls would be busy in the morning with breakfast for everyone and taking care of Sean and Carol, we thought it best to fill them in on our intentions for tomorrow. We explained everything we discovered and what we felt was the only alternative. I assured Sans that everything would be fine because CloBots would be the ones facing Empty. Steve was going to ride with the Chief of Police if he approved. And I was going to tag along with Bob Smalley. The girls seemed comfortable with our plans.

The kids fell asleep early while watching TV, and the four of us spent the rest of the evening relaxing and talking about old times.

We arrived at WOSE at precisely 8 A.M. and headed directly for the programming unit. WOSE has the best programmers in the world. With offensive programming in place it was a piece of cake to add defense to its capabilities. Defense, along with offense, would make the unit capable of defeating and destroying the enemy. We explained to the programmers just what we needed and they immediately went to work.

While we waited for the new program to be written, Steve and I grabbed some coffee and went looking for the Chief of Police and Bob Smalley. We found them both on opposite sides of the reception area, engrossed in magazines. We introduced ourselves to the Chief of Police who introduced himself as Garry Langston. I introduced Steve to Bob Smalley. Bob shook hands with Garry. We spent the next hour going over what we determined from our investigation of the CloBots. We also shared our plan of attack. They had a number of questions which we were able to give them a satisfactory answer. After they were satisfied concerning the situation, we, the four of us, headed to the warehouse to prepare a couple of CloBots.

I had brought hair and saliva samples from Sans and would provide whatever was needed of my own DNA. Within thirty minutes standing before us were duplicates of me and Sans. I am amazed every time I watch this process: a generic CloBot's face morphing into whomever, but even more so, when you see yourself appearing right in front of you. I didn't even have to ask Bob or Garry what they thought of what was happening: I could tell by the look of amazement on their faces.

About 3 P.M. we got word that the new program was finished and ready to be installed. By three-thirty we were ready to head out the door for home, my home, that is, with the two CloBots. Both Garry, with his men and Bob agreed to remain unseen as backup: they would keep the house under surveillance.

Chapter Twenty-eight
Implementing the Trap

Empty knew something was up by the multiple cars and police vehicles going into South Shores. His attention was peaked. He felt there was no need for a phone call. This was a time for action.

Boundaries maintain a social order in a kingdom. Systems are developed as boundaries. Ours has been recovered.

I was the second car to enter carrying the two CloBots. All others were unmarked cars and vans. All units parked a safe distance from the house at various locations on different streets. Since our house was on a corner it was readily visible from many angles and positions. There were even unmarked cars put into place earlier in the day by the Police Chief throughout the subdivision so that a concentration of cars in one area would not be suspicious.

The Chief also had the house wired earlier that day after we explained the plan. Steve and Garry were parked half way down the block directly in front of the house. Bob Smalley was to the west, several hundred yards down our street, Ocean View Place. I was to join him later after I got the CloBots set in place. We were set and ready to go a little after 6:25 P.M.

Empty approached the guard shack and asked for directions: he appeared to be lost. The guard stepped out and pointed up the street toward the north. Big mistake! One quick blow and he fell like a ton of bricks. It was nothing to snap his neck, like wringing out a wash cloth. CloBots are built with enormous natural strength: this enabled them to enact many types of capital punishment scenarios. Empty dumped the body into the guard shack and put the 'unattended' sign in the window.

There was a rap on the passenger's side window. Bob rolled down the window and said,

"Get in Hank."

The door opened but Bob was engrossed with texting his wife and did not look to see who got in. Finishing his text he turned to ask Hank if everything was ready.

Once again, the predator was about to confront his prey. Once again, the prey is unaware of the attack.

Bob never saw the knife that sliced him from ear to ear. Empty struck with the power and speed of a locomotive: the strike was precise and deadly. The predator was victorious.

There was a knock at the front door. On guard, Hank opened the door slowly expecting Empty to be the caller. But, much to Hanks surprise, there stood Bob Smalley, with the usual cigarette dangling from the side of his mouth.

The CloBot would not have known something was wrong. That is why I did not follow the plan we had set out. I had a few tweaks I thought would work out better. The first was to store Hank's CloBot in the closet: he could be let loose if needed. I had a better feeling about Empty's actions and could better set him up for the execution of our trap. So far! So good!

"What are you doing here Bob?" I asked.

"Garry thought you needed someone in here with you just in case you needed backup." Bob replied. "I just couldn't sit in the car and let you face that monster alone."

Intuition's first thought was "What's happening?" Bob doesn't know it's really me. He thinks that I am a Clobot. How would he know it is really me? I asked Bob,

"Weren't you supposed to stay in the car until you were signaled?" I was trying to get a handle on the change of plans.

"Well, you hadn't shown up yet and I got worried," Bob replied.

That made sense, except Bob is a polished veteran. Bob was in on the development of the plan and would stick to its scheme in order not to compromise its integrity. A plan compromised is a plan in jeopardy. Something was not right.

"Bob, go back to your post and I will be there in a couple minutes," I said trying to get back on plan.

"Can't do that! I need to be in here." Bob, sternly replied!

This confirmed it. This was not Bob, for he knew backup was not to come inside under any circumstances.

Empty just made mistake number one.

"We are fine, nothing is going to happen, Bob, just go home and I'll call you in the morning."

Bob started walking and looking around as if he were searching for something or someone. Then after a few minutes he turned and said,

"Well, it looks like we meet again."

I looked into his eyes and saw, not Bob, but the eyes of the cold-blooded killer I had seen seventeen years ago. And that cold, calculated, heartless voice again tried to mock me. Now standing before me was Robert "Empty" Jones. My creation of justice, the original RX, is now corrupted by evil.

However, this time, I was prepared!

"And, where is that pretty new little wife of yours? I'm sure you would love to introduce her to an old friend. You know, we go a long way back." He sneered.

"From what I remember, the way you treat women I don't think she has any desire to meet you. She, like Carol, is full of everything you are 'EMPTY' of." I sneered, right back.

Pulling out Bob's gun, Empty said,

"Enough of the cat and mouse. It's very clear who is in control here," thinking he had the same upper hand as he had in all his assaults, he continued, "I have something very special planned for the little misses, just like I had for your first wife," he sneered in a heavy, forceful voice. Then, reaching out and striking me across the face with the butt of the gun he demanded, "Now, call the misses or I'll just shoot you and go find her myself. But, I'm sure you don't want to miss the show….er, the 'rerun,' I should say."

At this point, Empty felt in full control, just as he had seventeen years ago. He was the master puppeteer pulling the strings, and we were to dance to his every whim. He remembered the horror and fear he had inflicted that night and once again, it was his craving. He could see what he thought was fear in my eyes.

Mistake number two: he mistook rage for fear!

I let him play his little game as long as possible till I knew I had pushed him to the point of no return. His anger was about to explode.

"Get her in here now!" He screamed.

It took every ounce of resistance in their bones not to respond to what they were hearing over the wiretap. Steve and the Chief of Police had to just sit there and not respond, along with all the other cops on stakeout who were wired. Steve and the Chief of Police also thought it had to be very hard for Bob Smalley and Hank, whom, they thought were just around the corner. They had no idea Bob was dead and Hank was the one facing Empty.

Turning toward the kitchen, I called out,

"Honey, an old friend would like to see you."

There was stirring in the kitchen. "Be right there," was the response.

The lights were much brighter in the kitchen compared to the track lighting in the living room. The figure in the doorway was difficult to recognize. Pausing to survey the situation, the Clobot then moved forward. With a slow, sultry, sexy stride she moved closer and closer, every step distinct and purposeful. With every step toward Hank and his guest she could see Empty's face beginning to change as her beautiful features became more and more visible.

What appeared to be nothing but raging lust seventeen years ago and what he was again prepared to ravage on Hank's second wife now had a look of incomprehension. Empty, either was having a hard time comprehending what was happening or could not believe what he was seeing. Stopping, toe to toe with Empty, in her most sexy voice and hot breath engulfing his face, she smiled and said,

"Hello, Mr. Jones….or, should I just call you Empty since we go a long way back?" She said, standing defiantly before him.

Mistake number three, thinking he was going to see Sans: this was not the second wife but it was Carol, Hank's first wife.

After arriving home I re-cloned the CloBot that had been cloned to be

Sans. I knew Carol would be the key to once again terminate Empty.

Three strikes and you're out!

Empty was totally stunned! He had flashbacks to the night he brutally assaulted and murdered her. These were thoughts of pleasure. But, there were more recent thoughts that overshadowed the pleasures he was enjoying from their first encounter. These thought revealed what had happened less than ten years ago. These were the thoughts of when Carol had executed him for that crime. These were thoughts of fear, horror, and pain as he was repeatedly stabbed to death.

Déjà vu replayed! Am I being redundant, again?

As I have said before, CloBots are built with great strength. And CloBot Carol, with the defensive programming that CloBot Empty did not have, had no trouble subduing her opponent. With a flash she reached out and grabbed him by the neck with one hand and knocked the gun out of his hand with the other. She then spun him around like a rag doll and threw him to the floor face down. Carol knew she had to remove the skull cap and tear out and destroy the electronic brain. The brain that had been compromised through a faulty seal by Empty's blood when he was first executed by Carol, the robot, just over nine years ago.

Empty tried to fight back but the first generation CloBot is no match for the second generation. All the while Carol was disabling her opponent, Empty, was re-experiencing the horrors of his capital punishment. The blood that had penetrated and compromised the Clobot that was used in Empty's execution now had the memories of that execution. Empty was experiencing, even in the body of a Clobot, the horror, fear, and pain he experience when he was executed.

Carol was able to easily remove the back portion of Empty's skull, just as she had practiced time and time again. She then took the hammer provided and smashed Empty's brains out, striking him over and over as she raised the hammer and then plunge it into Empty's skull cavity. Stabbing him over and over, just as he had done to her, only this time Carol was using a hammer instead of a knife. Carol was not too quick to end the destruction of Empty. Once again, she was able to inflict upon Empty everything she had experienced from this brutal animal when he attacked her. Once again, Empty was experiencing everything he felt when he had been executed. Carol was able to enact revenge. Empty was able to experience defeat.

Déjà vu to you, Empty!

When Carol was finished wreaking her revenge, the only thing visible when looking at the inside of Empty's head, was two battered, lifeless, empty eyes. Empty's perpetual "eye for an eye."

Double jeopardy? Never!

Capital Punishment, an eye for an eye? Forever!

"Rest in peace, my beloved Carol." I whispered.

"I love you Sans!"

The animal kingdom is steady as a rock. The human kingdom is built upon The Rock!

Epilogue

All first generation CloBots were recalled and the seals replaced. There is no possibility that a CloBot will ever be compromised again.

As a result of a new ad campaign assuring the people that all malfunctions in the CloBots have been corrected, without any possibility of this ever happening again, fear has once again become a thing of the past. And, so has crime.

Author

Tom Cooke, Born May 1940, Married 1959 (Wife Deceased after 59-1/2 Years Together). Three Children (Son Deceased) Two Daughters Still Prodding Their Dad, Ten Grandchildren & Twenty-Five Great-Grandchildren. Three Years USMC, Two Years College. Fifteen Years Office Work, 30 years Tile & Marble Contractor. Retired 2005.